A Pig Story
to Provoke Thinking

Alpha Lamb

PublishAmerica
Baltimore

Hardcover 978-1-4512-7966-5
Softcover 978-1-4512-7967-2
PUBLISHED BY PUBLISHAMERICA, LLLP
www.publishamerica.com
Baltimore

Printed in the United States of America

A Pig Story
to Provoke Thinking

Alpha Lamb

CHAPTER 1 ARRIVAL

Once upon a near-future time, there lives a pig which is kept as a pet by a human family. It is not clear why this family would keep a pig rather than a dog or a cat, which are more popular choices.

This pig is adopted by the family at a good age, young enough to pick up tricks swiftly, and old enough not to require nursery care. The couple in the family has been married for a year, with a newly-born soon after marriage. Not only do they love each other, but they are also generous enough to spread their love to whoever they would come across. Their female pet pig is so well treated and respected that their reference to there being four members in the family cannot be disputed. It is fed hygienic food not much below the quality that they would feed themselves, including minced meat and tofu. It is taken to animal hospital to have periodic check-up. Though sometimes reprimanded for bad behaviour, it has never been kicked. As far as pet goes, it should not find any reason to ask for more. Indeed, it receives almost as many hugs and kisses as the family baby girl. The housewife, also a free lance home architect, is glad that having two girls in the house gives her breaks and attention to her own professional interest, since the two girls like more to play with each other than with her. The newer girl, who addresses her as Mistress, demands less attention.

Soon after arrival, this pet is given the name Angel, a name worthy of any precious little human girl. True to her name, Angel, in her own way, spreads angelic blessings to touch anyone who can have the patience to bother about her. If you look lonely, she will stay by your side to keep you company. If you are miserable and sad, she will look you in the eye with understanding. She will try to comfort you and cheer you up, as if she has endless time in the world. Anyone who stays long enough knows that she has a heart of gold. It is not possible to stay angry with her for long. She is so pleasing and so pleasant. It can be said that she lights up your day.

It is a good time in human history. Sure, there are demonstrations and protests, hunger strikes, politics, and politicians, but there are no wars going on, not major wars anyway. Security, especially in travelling, is sometimes tight and sometimes not so tight. Master is away on business trips totalling slightly more than a month in a year. He knows a lot about the world outside, though not so much about what is happening in town. It is a good time, with shortcomings. As he would like to say: you cannot win them all.

It is also a time of advancement in information technology. Voice actuation has sent most keyboards to junk. Brainwave actuation has arrived. The gadget to be worn in your head is called the b-prompter. But there is a problem. You can order your tongue to speak what you want to be heard, but it is much more difficult to order your brain to think. If you hate someone, how can you be sure he has received the love message? Another problem is with security and privacy. If you cannot stop worrying, how can you be sure that worry will not be transmitted without your oversight? If you hate your boss, how can you stop telling him that when you say: Yes, Sir. Apparently it would be faster to use voice actuation than to check up your thought before sending it.

For a time, brainwave actuation appears to be going the way of the supersonic passenger aeroplane, a dead end in technological progress. Then someone has an idea. If my b-prompter sits forever as an ornament on the coffee table, why do I not put it on my pet? It works. It appears that my pet is almost as smart as I am. It can respond to the doctor's questioning when taken to animal hospital, and to my message too. You want me to take you for a walk now? I am busy. If you leave me alone for an hour, I shall just do that, alright? This is a win-win resolution for both of us. I am glad you understand.

What most people do not realise at this point in time is how consequential the impact of the b-prompter can have on animals in general, and pets in particular. Negligence of this proportion has happened before in human history, and no doubt will continue to happen. The switch, from eye contact and signalling to brainwave transmission, is no less than a quantum jump in intercommunication between human and animal. As expected, initially such intercommunication takes place mostly between pet and pet owner. How it will affect non-pet animal at a later stage is another story which may reward some future novel writer well. Be that as it may, it must be evident that past generations of pet and pet owner would have been green with envy if they could foresee the future.

The gadget is expensive, especially when you have it pre-ordered to fit your pet. It is difficult to explain why some owners would be prepared to spend so much money on their pets in stead of on themselves. Don't ask me. I am not a pet owner.

The pet gadget catches on, and Angel is soon wearing one. Cute or ugly, it becomes a permanent feature of what she looks, even in her sleep. She matures faster than the kid, and in turn is able to brainwave at an earlier age.

She knows soon after arriving that, though she is identified as a member of the family, she is not of the same kind. There is none of her kind in the neighbourhood. In the street, as Master says, it is a dog's world out there. She soon learns that it is a human world everywhere, including in the street.

This realization does not begin immediately. She always thinks she is no different from the earlier-arrived family kid, who also crawls on all fours. Both need caring, and both cannot be understood by the adults when they speak. Furthermore, both can make the adults happy or annoyed, and both cannot understand why this is so.

One day, it happens. Looking at the bathroom mirror after a bath, she can see three living characters. She glances at Master and Mistress. There is no question that they are exact copies, but who is that creature by their side? Wait a minute. This creature seems to copy my every move. I open my mouth, and it copies me instantaneously. I turn my head, and I cannot see it at all. Apparently, this creature only lives in the mirror. I should tell them about my discovery. There are five in the family. Hold on. How about the two adult copies? There should be seven, not five, right? I should tell them, but it appears that they have known about that already, since they do not look surprised. Is it possible they cannot see what I can see?

She has the chance to glance at the mirror when the family kid is also around, gradually reaching the conclusion that there are eight characters, including three pairs of identical twins such that one twin will be real and the other will stay inside the mirror. In addition, one guy will stay there. Then there is me, a real me.

She thinks about this phenomenon for some time. If that creature in the mirror moves exactly like me, it is more than my shadow in the sun. It is my identical twin. It must be. If Master and Mistress look exactly the same as their identical twins in the mirror, I must look the same too. This is how I look to them, and this is how I look to everybody else. If only I have eyes outside my body, I would have seen how I look like.

With time, she comes to the conclusion that the creature, her identical twin, is not alive in the sense that it can get out of the mirror. She finally picks up the courage to ask Mistress, at the risk of showing stupidity. Is the twin only a reflection? Is it not real and alive? Mistress would smile. It is not real. She would continue to marvel at the mirror as a wonderful human invention. It can tell how one looks, without one's ability to look at oneself. If she has such different features from the rest of the family, she must also be of a different kind. This realization is disturbing for some time. Then she grows to accept what cannot be changed.

The next puzzle is on her age. The family kid is born on Earth Day, but what is my birthday? Adult seldom appreciates how embarrassing it can be for a kid to forget his age. They like to ask: How old are you, even though they have asked the same boring question yesterday. Apparently they do not feel embarrassing to be so forgetful. A kid may deliberately refuse to give the known answer, but if he scratches his head, the adult will make fun of him. How can life be so unfair? Perhaps this is the first time when a kid learns that adults will not be fair to them.

She presses on Mistress. Please tell me how old I am. I really need to know. Master says that they can approach a geneticist to determine her age to within a month, but it is expensive and really not worthwhile. Why not fabricate a date? Nobody will know whether you are making it up or not. The family kid has a birth certificate, and you do not have one, but what does it matter? Many adopted human children do not know their birthday either. Mistress says no. You should never lie to a kid, and never let them know you are lying. It is the worst education. The kid will follow your bad example. Don't think about that again.

Instead, they decide to tell the truth. The family kid is not adopted like you. We gave birth to her. That is why she calls us Mom and Dad. She arrived the first day when she was born. She came out of the belly of Mistress. You came out of your mother's belly too. We are truly sorry. We do not know your mother, or when she gave birth, but we can be sure that she looks like you, and you like her. We shall always treat you and the kid equally, as a part of our family. Both of you are our loving girls.

She first sees her own kind on television. They call us pigs. So I am a pig, and they are humans. The pigs I can see are in groups. They live in a large pig factory. They are fed collectively. They are fatter than me, and yet they look hungry, hungry enough to have such poor table manner. They are not wearing this gadget. I wonder what is on their mind. If only I can communicate with them. To do so, of course, proves to be no more than wishful thinking. She soon comes to the conclusion that, unlike her, they are not kept as pets. What are they doing in the factory?

Being playful as ever, she is growing up fast, faster than the family kid. Though the equivalent of a pre-teen human girl, she finds the need to start being independent. The self-imposed need develops subconsciously. Mistress can be that busy, especially when Master is away, that I have to help her. I should not add to her trouble. I must take care of myself, because I am a big girl now.

The family kid is attending day care. She is not at home to play with her now. She can play with Mistress, but it is not the same thing. It takes time for her to get used to the change, though Mistress does not appear to be a bit disturbed. Indeed, Mistress seems to enjoy it more this way. She must learn to leave Mistress alone in her architectural practice. It is a quiet life in the morning, so quietly it can be frightening. Often, she spends time in the backyard, chasing butterflies and birds, and playing make-believe. She watches spiders weave webs, and waits for flowers to grow from day to day. How amazing it is that the bud seems to be frozen forever, and next morning it can be in full bloom. I wonder what happens at night, when I am asleep. She starts thinking about nature as defined in the backyard. Soon her thinking is extended to another field. Mistress says she is an architect. It means sitting there the whole morning drawing up things. Does she not find that boring? I can see that she is focussing attention. I must not disturb her. There must be something in whatever she is doing that can be so interesting. I wish I can know. I should ask her.

"Mistress, I want to be like you. I want to be an architect when I grow up."

"It is a good thought. But it is not that easy. It is especially difficult for you, being a pig."

"Why?"

"Most architectural structures are designed for human usage. They may not like to have them designed by non-human."

"Do you mean they will discriminate against me?"

"It is not a matter of discrimination, strictly speaking. Put it this way. They will have not that much confidence in a designer who will not be using the building the way humans will use it. What I mean is that pig and human can have different requirement from a building. You see, a pig farm or pig house is different from a human house."

"But we live in the same house. What is the difference whether it is designed by a pig or a human? The house will still fit all of us in."

"Usually there are more humans than pigs in the house. Take our example. There are three humans and there is only you. Take an art gallery. There are many more human visitors than pig visitors."

"They cannot say I am not good because there is less like me, can they?"

"You are right. It is a prejudice, but you cannot stop them acting according to their prejudice."

"I shall convince them that I can make good design, for human and for pig use."

"No doubt you will, but if they have no confidence in you, they will not give you the job."

"It is not fair. They cannot do that. No job for me because of my look. I shall challenge them, and make them change their mind. Will you help me?"

"Of course I would. I am a girl like you once upon a time. I am older now, and they call me woman, which means an older girl. One of these days we girls would fight together as good friends. We shall call each other comrades, meaning fellow fighters."

"Why do they make us fight them? Why can they not be right from the beginning? Are they stupid or something?"

"They used to look down on us. They think we are inferior to man, like your Master. They still do, though less so."

"Why would they do a thing like that? Master would not look down on you."

"He would not, and I bet he dares not. If he does, would you be on my side?"

"Of course, Mistress. I shall bring the baby girl along too. We girls will stand together to fight him until he yields."

"Good."

"What else is it that they have been unfair to us?"

"They used to not allowing us to vote, and they thought we are too stupid to become surgeons. They imprisoned us in the house. They have even forced us to wrap up like living mummies so that we can only see through slits in the cloth. Those basta …! We shall fight them with our teeth and nails. We shall make them beg for mercy."

Angel steals a glance at Mistress, whose wet eyes staring at some far away distance show that she is thinking of the past or future, not the present. Angel smiles as she visualizes those piteous creatures running for cover each in their mother's lap. It is going to be brutal. Promise you will never do it again.

"Still, it will be a hard life for you, being an architect. I know. I have been there before. Why not choose something easier, like writing novels."

"There is no law against pig being architect, is there?"

"No, but the obstacle is almost insurmountable. First you have to attend an architectural school, and there is a strong likelihood that they will not let you in because of your look. Next you have to be indentured by a mentor, and be employed in a professional firm. You cannot become one entirely by practising at home. There are so many obstacles for you to get an architectural license."

"I do not care about licence. I can be your assistant. We can work together to design great buildings and landscape."

"We can, but someday you will not be satisfied but to become an architect in your own right. Someday I will retire."

"I can help another architect then. You have many friends. You can tell me who to work with."

"It can be done, but other people may not take your ideas, even though such ideas are better than any that they can ever have. I know you are a creative and ambitious girl. You deserve much more than being an assistant all your life."

"Can I be an architect without building anything, like giving idea and comment on what is good and what is not good cnough?"

"You can become an architectural critic. You can make creative contribution. However, if you have never designed anything that has its significance in being built, why would anyone respect your criticism? This is especially so if they know you are a pig. I know it is unfair, but they can be biased against you, even though they may not admit being so."

"But they do not have to know that I am a pig."

"Before they read the writing, they want to know who you are, what have you done, and so on. Otherwise what you write will not get published, and what you say will not be heard. You will be wasting your time. It is like writing an unpublished novel."

"Who knows what will happen in future. Suppose after all these difficulties are overcome, do you think I still have a good future in this profession?"

"Not much. First of all, you client base will be limited in the human world. You know what client base is? It is people who will give you jobs. Secondly, they may only assign you projects substantially animal-oriented, like pig factory, slaughterhouse, horse stable, or cow stall."

"I hate those ugly buildings. I would never design a slaughterhouse. I wish all slaughterhouses are torn down."

"I know. I would still advise you to choose another career. Architecture is not a generous profession anyway. The pay is not good. Look at me. We live in a small house, and we fly economy."

"I do not care so much about pay, like you. I want job satisfaction."

"There are so many good professions around for you to choose from. Some can give very good job satisfaction too. Of course it is up to you to say whether there is satisfaction or not. I only want you to have a good life."

"I do not fancy writing novels. They are not real. I don't believe in making up things. It is like cheating."

"Look at it this way. Novels need imagination, which is not cheating. Imagine a future when pig and human are equal, when you are welcomed to become an architect like any human kid. That is good, isn't it? Some of us read your novel. They will say, "Hey, it is a good idea. Why do we not make that happen?" You know why man and woman are equal today? It is because some women in the past could imagine it. Then we fought for it until we won."

"Tell me more."

"It is a long story. You are a brave and persistent girl. Your turn will come. I am sure you can win your fights."

Without saying it out, Angel wants to assure Mistress: I shall not disappoint you. I shall be a fighter like you, and I shall never surrender, because no one can shut my face, even if he is much smarter than me. Not even if he is God.

Master returns home with a bruised forehead from an undeveloped country. It is politically correct, and safer, to call that an underdeveloped country, or a developing country. Why offend when you can avoid. Perhaps a better term is 'a great future developed country'.

"What happened?"

"I fell when chased by the police. I am sorry, Honey. I have not told you details on the telephone because I did not want you to be worried. It was only a minor injury. I did not even go to hospital."

"You should be more careful. Remember you are a family man."

"I know, but do you know what they are trying to do? It is outrageous. They want to introduce this new law to lock up woman in her own home. Not just retaining them at home, but locking them up in chain. They call it house arrest for moral misconduct. I can never stand that. It makes my blood boil."

"I know. I have seen the news. They had a few women in prison-wear declaring to prefer it that way, saying their freedom of choice to stay home cannot be denied."

"These women are a disgrace. They may be paid or forced to do so."

"I don't know, but let us give them the benefit of the doubt."

"They say they have the nation's support since the majority remain silent. We are accused to be the trouble-making minority."

"I hate these sour pickles. How can they say silence means yes? It is so preposterous. Silence means nothing until the proposal is responded by word or by expression."

"Silence means wait a minute. If silence lasts, it may mean: Go to hell, without making the offence by saying it out. It may mean embarrassment on what is private to me, or that I despise your question so much as not to honour it with an answer."

"We women should never be taken for granted. This arrogance of assumption is bondage on both sexes. We are all victimised. Let us be clear: Silence means silence."

"I know, Honey. I love you, and I shall never force anything on you because of your silence."

"By the way, how is your local partner?"

"He was beaten in the head. They detained him for a day. Those pigs are violent."

Mistress tightens her lips as she stares at him sternly. Angel at first cannot understand. They have pigs in the police too? Then she realizes the remark is derogatory. Angel has never seen pigs in the police. They have ferocious dogs, but not pigs.

"He is alright now, but his neighbour is in big trouble. Their girl is raped."

"Oh dear! Have they napped the rapist?"

"There is proof that the girl was choked. She claimed to have fainted, but she could not prove it to the doctor. They suspected she was seducing the rapist while enjoying every moment awake."

"How could they? What do they expect her to do?"

"She is supposed to defend her honour with her life. Everyone there knows that being new and untouched is essential to a girl in the marriage market. There is no major wound on her body to show that she has put up more than symbolic resistance. She is now accused of corroding an honourable fellow citizen, she has pleaded guilty, and she has agreed to home imprisonment."

"I cannot believe it."

"She is now in house arrest, to be handcuffed all through the day. This will educate other girls not to follow her example. Neighbouring countries may follow the practice. I hate these pigs."

Master wants to withdraw what has slipped out of his mouth for the second time, but it is too late.

"I mean: they are not real pigs. Most pigs are good. These are the bad apples."

"How did this police brutality happen to you? Tell me. Did they not give any warning at all?"

"They tried to give loud warning on an organ, but the organ refused to function. They used their truncheons on whoever was in their way. They claimed the use is judicious."

"That reminds me of your dirty ditty: There is a policeman, whose organ refuses to function. Cheaters they are. I know. This is not funny, but I just cannot help it."

Master seems to have second thought.

"We cannot blame the police entirely for chasing us demonstrators and beating us up. They are only taking order. It is in their job. If not, they may get sacked, and brutality may be used against them. You know how far these countries can go."

"I don't care. Nobody can do such things with a clear conscience."

"They have high unemployment rate out there. People have to eat, but I agree with you on their guilty conscience."

"I hate these pigs...pickles."

It is Master's turn to stare at Mistress, as both steal a glance at Angel, who briefly takes offence. Why should they associate everything ugly with us pigs? It is high time to stop this stigmatization. Fortunately, hers is of the forgiving type. It is alright. It is just a matter of speech that they are used to. They will change their look on us with time. I hope one of these days I shall win a beauty contest against human girls.

Mistress is up in the floor above, clearing Master's luggage and turning the tap on, with the intention of joining at the bath to clean him up. Her smile at Master before she goes leaves no doubt on what she has approved and is pleased with.

Angel cannot help wondering how a layback nonchalant guy like Master can mingle and fit in with those hotheads and rabble rousers on the television screen. She is not aware that many of the silent majority just off screen consist of reluctant fellow walkers and latecomers driven by the challenge to their basic decency. Some of them will remain passive until their blood has reached boiling point. The challenge to stand up is the last hurdle to keep authority and authoritarianism at bay in their ferocious bite on the public conscience.

She has waited to speak to Master. Now is a good time.

"You are brave."

"I did what I have to do. I shall do it again."

"Are you a feminist?"

"It all depends on what a feminist is. No, I do not consider myself to be one, though I do believe a woman should not be stopped to become whatever a man can become. Any job restriction is discriminatory. Equal right must be for all. You think that a certain woman is not strong enough for the job? Fine, don't give her the job. It can happen to a man too. Open the job vacancy to all who are strong enough. I believe woman can go as far as man can. If man can be God, woman can be God too."

"Isn't that feminism?"

"You can say that, but it is more. Call that universalism if you like."

"Are you doing this demonstration for Mistress and for all us girls?"

"Look. Mistress is free now, but she is not free until all women are free. Freedom is not divisible. We cannot be free until every one of us is free."

Angel recalls having heard this before. She did not understand then, nor would she understand it now. Is Mistress free or not? She tells herself not to forget what Master has just said, and to think about it later. She nods her head. Me too! I am free but I am not free until all pigs are free. How about that? It is meaningful and well said. It has depth.

"What is rape?"

"It is like a man beating up a woman without reason. If you insist, he may give enjoyment as the reason, or he may say it is human nature for him as a man."

"Just like saying: I like it, so what? How would you like me doing the same to you? This man must be crazy."

He seems reluctant to explain further. I shall learn more about what it means in the library. When I grow up, I can be a defence lawyer, and I shall defend that poor girl in that crazy country, free of charge. How can she be so stupid to plead guilty and to accept imprisonment? She makes herself a disgrace to us all. They can always say, "If she can, why not you?" I would fight them with every drop of my blood, for our sake even if not for mine alone. I wonder how long she will be home imprisoned.

"Imprisonment is only a small part of her big problem. She has brought shame to the family. Would you like to marry this cheap, soiled, and used merchandise as your fourth wife? No thanks. You go ahead. No marriage means that she would have no chance to be raped again, except possibly at home by visitors. If so, she has less chance to argue for not being responsible. One way out for the family is honour killing. It is their neat way to get rid of the problem which she has brought along."

Angel does not understand what honour killing is. Is it an honour for the poor girl to be killed, or is it an honour for others affected by her? She does not choose to ask Master. She will look it up in the dictionary.

"I hope she will be out of prison soon?"

"It makes little difference to her. She will never be accompanied out of the house, because anyone accompanying her will feel ashamed. She can never be out alone."

"Out alone just like me?"

"Not exactly. You are young, and we are concerned about your safety outside. She would not be allowed out alone anyway as an adult, even if she has not been raped. She needs protection anywhere away from home."

"Why? Boys can be out alone, but not girls."

"The say it is their culture, and they will defend their culture anywhere in the world. It is absolutely bulls ..."

Master apparently has difficulty swallowing what must have smelled terrible. Angel cannot understand. What have bulls got to do with it? If there is a demonstration, I do not mind being a bull leading the storm against the barrier. One of these days, I am going to go farther than Master. I shall make these pickles bleed. Forgive me, Mistress, for not taking your advice to have an easy life.

Gradually, she can see the picture more clearly. Raped or not, that girl is no more than a glass decorative vase on the shelf. She will spend most of life on the shelf, and can only be moved by hand-carrying. She should refuse even if the hand says: Go ahead and make your own move. If she is cracked, it has to be her fault as the trouble maker. Since there is no market for broken glass which cannot be fixed even by crazy glue, her family has to take the trouble getting rid of the shards by honour killing. The neighbour cat is allowed to roam freely, but not their woman, who is weaker and needs more protection.

Master being back, once in a while Mistress would take either her or the family kid, but never both, along to distribute pamphlet and meeting invitation door to door. 'Don't make-believe you are the Creator. Animals have rights too.' Some respond rudely, though most would welcome them with a smile, and some would even give chocolate to the girl who remains silent on the side, waiting in the cold for the conversation to end. Good girl. Angel can now understand what this is all about. One of those rights concerns her becoming an architect, or even a defence lawyer.

Her architectural dream lingers on for a while, before fading away. What better advice can there be, especially from a practising professional architect, one that cares so much for her? Hopefully those pamphlets and meetings would bring along good helpful changes in the future. Being a pet for life is not an option. She knows little about other professions. In any case, she is yet too young to devote too much thought on her career.

The sense of unfairness surfaces every now and then. She envies those human kids, who can have so many openings. Then she hears a verse from a song: 'Some are lucky; some are not. I am thankful for what I got.' Yes, I should be thankful that I am luckier than most pigs. They say life is never supposed to be fair. I know. We are never born to be equal. It is hard luck, but I must accept reality with grace, as they would say.

From the age of innocence, she has arrived at the age of contentment, bitter as it may be. Pig and other animals are born unequal to human. At least that is what they think. Wait a minute. Nobody can deny what I want to think. If someone tells me to think in a particular way because of my look, I shall simply ignore him. I would not even bother to tell him what I am thinking, now that I know how to turn off the b-prompter. I enjoy thinking, and I shall be a thinker when I grow up. In fact, I do not even have to wait, because I have already started. Mistress wants me to have an easy life. What can be easier than thinking?

She does not know, until much later, that thinking is not easy at all. It should have been much easier to have her future making failed attempts to become an architect. She would have not been so lonesome, and so frustrated.

It should not happen, but it has happened. She is taken for a walk on a sunny spring afternoon, when this smelly pig is pushed and jostled along towards her. From the evening news, she learns that the beast earlier has escaped from the slaughterhouse.

A strike is going on in the slaughterhouse. On television, she can now clearly see what a slaughterhouse is like. There are carcasses on hangers, blood stains on the floor, and hooks on butchery tables. It makes her sick. That night there is talk in the family. Pork is going to be expensive. Luckily, we have stocked up.

The defining moment comes when she learns that pork is meat from pig. She already knows that human considers eating human flesh a serious degrading crime. Why? Cannibalism is the term used for describing an animal eating its own kind. They call human meat flesh, just as they call pig meat pork, and cow meat beef. What is wrong with eating flesh? Until this moment, I am not abhorrent to pork as in minced pork. There must be something degrading eating meat of your own kind. Would I eat my own leg when I am hungry? I must be going crazy. I am degraded by what I have been fed. Why have they done this to me?

Suppose I stop eating pork from this minute on. But I cannot find that much difference between minced pork, minced beef, and minced chicken. Shall I make an agreement with cows, saying that if you do not eat my kind, I shall not eat your kind too? It is fortunate for humans. They can eat any animal, but no animal can eat them. Do they make it a crime because they have so much to choose from other than their own flesh? Yet I have heard of them dying of hunger, even if human flesh is at hand. They must be taking that degradation very seriously. Am I too inferior to have such a feeling?

The very next week after this pork eating thought entanglement, she is converted to be a vegetarian for life. She has debated briefly with Mistress beforehand, but the decision is her to make, and is given due respect.

Master comes back from the trip, surprised by Angel's sudden conversion. He is in a joking mood, taking notice only after Mistress has winked twice, but he still cannot appreciate the sensitiveness involved with Angel around. It takes a long explanation at bedtime.

The vegetarian conversion marks another juncture in Angel's life. It is a pity, or even sad, that her age of innocence can be so short, and her age of contentment so transitory. Had she not been a pig, she would still be budding in schoolyards and playgrounds. She would be dreaming of being a policeman one day, a fireman the next, and a postman delivering greetings. She would be like a girl listening to stories of princess and castle, and how the evil dragon throwing out fire would be killed. That girl would close her eyes fully, and would suddenly say as her Daddy is about to slip quietly out of her bedroom: Daddy, can you tell me the story one more time?

There is no turning back from this critical juncture. It is like in the Book of Genesis, when Eve has bitten the apple. Suddenly everything is so clear. To know is to be tormented. The b-prompter is the apple, bringing her the loss of innocence, a loss that neither she nor Eve could have imagined. The bite of the apple and the wearing of the b-prompter follow Murphy's Law. But for that law, Eve, the apple, and the snake could have lived happily ever after, and so would Angel, the b-prompter, and the other family members. The Book of Genesis would have been thin with not more than a few pages. The Bible would have no more content than an unfinished first chapter. I would be sound asleep by now. My suffering readers would also be spared their time and expense. It is apparent that we overlook that law at our own cost. Goodbye to the Garden of Eden, a history that can only be remembered wistfully.

After Murphy's Law kicks in, she falls sick for no apparent reason. The sickness has gone away, but not the feeling of sickness. Ever so often, she wants to be left alone to be immersed in that feeling. Her thought wanders, sometimes out of control. She remains a jolly good fellow, giving blessings whenever and to whoever she can. Her melancholy mood may come as quickly as it goes. Her laughter can be evaporated away so quickly as to be frightening. It makes you think that you might have done something or have said something wrong to her.

She has arrived. Her epic journey is about to begin. Her lifelong search, initially for herself as a pet pig, will gradually expand to cover all animals in the human world. Her journey can be likened to a Greek tragedy, with her being a plaything of the gods. Footprints have been marked ahead for her to follow. She may be allowed to stray a little, but never too much. It is not that she can propose and God will dispose, because the proposal has already been made for her. She is like a swimmer, wet from head to toe and up to the neck in water. All she can do is to swim hard to reach the other unseen shore. There will be nothing in between shores for her to hold on. Her destiny has been predetermined. She resides, and fate decides.

Life goes on as before. She does not know yet, but soon she will have more worries ahead, though this does not necessarily make things worse. As one worry weighs on top of another, the resultant weight is not a matter of simple addition, because the top will serve to lighten the bottom. The worrying mind is apparently able to adjust itself. This is a saving grace.

CHAPTER 2 MOTHERHOOD

Angel is pregnant. It is a strange experience, starting with symptoms of hunger, indigestion and listlessness. All of a sudden, out of the middle of nowhere, she yearns to eat some particular food. Sometimes the yearning goes away, and sometimes it changes. Her smell is playing trick with her. There is this funny smell around, but I cannot find out where it comes from. Her mood swings too, sometimes to a point where the pleasing and comforting Angel cannot be found.

Her pregnancy comes accidentally, during a visit less than two hours driving distance away. The family couple they visit is related. Each family also happens to keep a pig as a pet. Because of their common interest, the two families often exchange interesting conversation, and in the process mutually benefit from the experience and share the joy. They may have influenced each other to keep a pig in the first place.

It was sheer pleasure for Angel alone to be with this male pig around her age. Unlike Angel, he is illiterate, the happy-go-lucky sort who will die laughing whether he is going to heaven or hell. He is the perpetual joker and clown who cannot be pinned down. There are no such terms as commitment and responsibility in his dictionary, if he ever has one. Charge him with a job, and he will come back every five minutes: it is your turn. Discuss an issue with him, and he will pretend to be serious in one minute, but the next minute he will turn the issue into a joke. He is that hopeless.

Clearly he and Angel are in diametrically opposite ends, intellectually speaking. It is not that he is not smart. He is, no doubt. It is a wonder how Angel can get along with him, but get along they can, and very well too. Can it be that Angel has left her brain at home? There is no better explanation. She may be stooping down to his level, but if she does, you can see that she is enjoying every moment.

It is a safe bet her enjoyment will not last. Sooner or later, she will find this boy unbearable. His jokes are childish, and snappish like firecracker. Give him a slice of cake to eat, and he would enjoy more by smashing it into someone's face, and even more if everybody does the same. Certainly, he has no depth. Yet no one can admit that he can make you laugh, short and forgetful as the laughter can be. Perhaps she would find him unbearable had they been together for a few days more.

In her mind, she will always recall the short stay as the happiest time in her life. She would say to herself: Life can be that happy, and like him you can be that happy too, if only you can cast away whatever there is in your mind. Later in life, she will even pray converted to be like him, a simpleton and free spirit, slick as river mud, ever to escape from your fingers however hard you try holding it on. It is mud that can dance in any current in any direction.

No one watching them cannot help but share their joy. They run around, playing catch-me-if-you-can, hide-and-seek, and mock fighting. They try to climb on each other's back. They roll over, jump up, crawl, and scratch hard on the soil below. Then they scratch each other. You scratch my back, and I shall scratch yours in turn. They push against each other to see who will be the first to fall, and falling down can be so much fun, accompanied by so much laughter.

For Angel, it is a sensation completely different from playing with the family kid. No doubt he would feel the same way too. It is like playing with your own shadow, except that this time the shadow has materialized to have a will-power of its own, to dance on its own, and to speak what you want to hear. Unlike the family kid, this male shadow can move and run to please by what she wants to be pleased. How can that be? Suddenly she has the answer. He is her kind. They are of the same kind. She is not alone in the world. She is not unique. Who wants to be unique anyway?

Suddenly it happens. They are starting to mate. Both of them have never known mating before, or afterwards, but it happens, as if nature has a helping hand to guide them along. What is the implication of mating, and what is the consequence? No such questions exist on their mind, let alone the answers. It is just a game, a game with great fun.

It starts with the game of tickling. As they chase to tickle each other, laughing all the time, the chase is interrupted to catch breath. Exhaustion is not a problem. It seems they have endless energy in reserve. Then he starts to climb on her back, holding tight. He will not spare her. She will not be able to get away this time. She is panting to catch her breath, ready to shake him off the next minute. Then this tickling feeling spreads. It is such a deep feeling that for a moment she holds her breath while remaining motionless. The moment becomes timeless. The feeling spreads far and wide. It becomes so strong that she wants to say: Stop. Just hold it there. Not so fast. Let me enjoy it, and let me focus so I can remember what it is like afterwards. She stops laughing. She becomes very serious suddenly. Then she feels the pain, a pain accompanied by such sweetness that she cannot tell which is which. She feels so full and complete as if her body is ready to explode. She lets out a scream so loud that it would frighten anyone nearby. Help. I am dying. Someone hold my heart please. It is trying to jump out of my body. Let me die. I want nothing more.

If she does die, it will definitely be the sweetest death there is ever on Earth, but she does not die, of course. The bliss that seems eternal does not last that long. She is now exhausted, as she has never been so exhausted before. She can lie down now. Whoever behind her she cannot remember, or care. It is all so quiet, but not for long. Her snorting starts, growing strong so very quickly as if she is forcing it up. It is a wonder how fast she can fall into a dream. It is a sweet dream of heaven, with light so bright as to dazzle the eyes to see only foggy outlines. Music is in the air. It is soft music, more like a lullaby sung by a mother to her baby. When she wakes up, she finds herself wet through with sweat, but try as she may, she cannot remember what the dream is about.

He is lying by her side, watching meaningfully. She wonders why he can have changed so quickly from that funny jester. Something must have happened to him. Then she watches him speak.

"You have made me so happy."

"Hush. Don't say a word."

"I mean it, truly."

She does not want to hear any joke and laughter from him at this moment. Without her explanation, he understands. He is not that shallow after all. As she feels him lying close by her side, she can see a breeze trying to rustle leaves. Is that low crisp whisper real, or is it her imagination? She imitates the whisper, making the sound so light that she cannot even hear it herself.

She feels his hand patting on her shoulders. She whispers into the grass: Slower. Good. More slowly please. Her back is like a bed of pebbles kissed by eiderdown, all the way from shoulders to toes, and reverse course after a brief stop. There is no knowing whether the crystal-clear water in a spring brook touches the pebbles or not. It may be flying above, breathing coolly down. Her body feels so smooth and light that it dances with the rhythm and follow the lead in harmony. She closes her eyes. There is absolutely nothing she wants from this world now. Just leave me alone, in peace, all by myself. I am fully fulfilled.

She recalls this mating scene for years afterwards. It is one of those lifetime things. She knows that she can never have it again, even if she can meet the same boy. They never meet again. Sometimes she wonders what the human experience is like. More likely, they can do better, what with their sex education and preparedness, both psychological and physical. Theirs can be more romantic, which means playing in the dark or something. What have they got to hide from broad daylight? They may have appliances to help along too. Then she relaxes her thought. Mine may not be the best, but why should I go for your best, or compare you against me. You get on with your life, and I get on from what I shall always cherish, and return to from time to time.

The trip is over. Her pregnancy is discovered by Mistress, who as usual is most helpful to allay her fear and confusion. It is not that Mistress knows everything, even though she has been a mother before. After all, what applies to human may not apply to pig. Ever warm-hearted, Mistress is diligent enough to search for information from friends and on the internet at her own spare time, which cannot be much. What is pregnancy? It means you are having babies. They will grow inside your body. Babies are just like you, except they are tiny little ones, so tiny that you can almost blow them away. They look like you when you were young, but far younger than you can remember. They will depend on you for everything, and they will be around you forever.

For a while, Master and Mistress are kept busy. Master, a not-so-good though hard-working handy-man, builds a new contraption for her future expansion. Mistress cleans up the mess left behind by her. They have always been nice to her. Now they are even nicer, to the point that she often regrets her demand and dependence on them. Indeed, she sometimes feels sorry for them. They seem to understand well what she as a potential pig mother is going through, but do they really?

"Do not worry. Just relax. It is not your fault."

"Have I done something wrong? How can I get rid of it?"

"My sweet Angel, do not even think about that. You will be a happy mother soon. This will be over before you know. We are all very happy for you, and we shall do whatever we can. We are with you all the way."

"You mean there is a new one in the family?"

"Yes, little ones will come out of your body, and they will look like you, but much smaller than you."

"Where will it come out?"

"No, it does not come out of your mouth. It will come out from behind you. This is called birth. I have to warn you, though. It can be painful, but not for long. They will call you Mother, just like what my kid would call me."

Angel begins to suspect that there is some difference between human and pig in giving birth. She hopes that there is another pig around to talk to. It would have been best if that is some pig with the experience of pregnancy, but she is ready to settle for one even without the experience, someone of her kind that does not have to do anything but listen to her. She is that desperate. Sometimes she feels herself all alone in the forest floor, with a painful though invisible wound, as the family together with queer animals circling around her trying but not knowing how to help. Then she sees herself in the pig factory, but there is no pig there. Cattle, goats, and even chicken, but no pigs.

It is a difficult pregnancy, difficult for everyone around her but especially for her. The birth that follows is extremely painful. The couple stay up all night, with blankets and hot water. What a mess! Master is ordered around, often in a hurry, and she can hear Mistress shouting, amid her own groaning and screaming. It is so painful that she prays for anything to stop it, even death. She is so tired that she wants to sleep, but she cannot sleep. It goes on, each time more painful, and each time so unbearable that she cannot believe the pain can be any worse, but it gets worse each time.

Motherhood from pregnancy is a metamorphosis, similar to butterfly evolving from caterpillar. Like most mothers, Angel is caught totally unprepared, both physically and mentally. It is not that Mistress does not try her best to prepare and educate Angel, but it proves to be an extremely thankless task, like teaching a caterpillar how to fly. Yet there can be some common ground and familiar terrain, since both can find the same tree with the same leaves and flowers. Beyond that, there is not available a single guide post, let alone a road map, for Angel as a pig mother, blindly groping an elephant. There is no option but to have the patience to keep on groping and drawing conclusions which would have to be reviewed and repeated continually. Apparently, the dictate of nature is the only guide.

There is no question that the transformation from girl to pregnancy to motherhood is a baptism of fire. The challenging demand, which comes so quickly as not to allow catch of breath, is that everything else must be put on hold. Gone is the free spirit in the girl, perhaps forever. If pregnancy is the equivalent of war declaration, motherhood must be like enemy invasion at the castle gate, or Stalingrad. Everything that can be sacrificed has to be sacrificed to defend motherland. You can say it is unfair to the mother. You can say motherhood is invasive selfishness by a breeding entity. You can say whatever you feel, but it cannot be denied that motherhood is a way of life. Fatherhood does not even come close in intensity. I know. The difference must arise from not having gone through pregnancy and giving birth, or something else beyond our comprehension.

Piglets are born. Tiny little muddles of flesh that do not move at first. Only two survive. The rest are taken away, though not immediately. She has never seen them since. Mistress says they are in heaven.

She is so tired she keeps on sleeping, for how many days she does not know. When she wakes up, she finds herself in some contraption of a big box on the sitting room floor. No one is around. With an empty mind, she keeps quiet. It has been a hazy dream, but reality creeps in. Slowly she remembers what she has gone through. The pain is still there, as if from a wound slowly healing from below. She realizes that it is all over for her now, and for the couples whom she has given so much trouble. She controls herself. Calm descends, until a stroke of thunder knocks on her head, like all mother waking up from a long sleep immediately after giving birth. Where are my babies?

She shouts loudly. Mistress is shocked from her absorbing work on the electronic drawing board. She rushes in, almost suffering a fall. Are you alright, Angie Dear? I am sorry not being with you, but your babies are with me close by. No, I am not taking your babies away. It is never my intention, thank God. I am just keeping a close watch on them while you are sleeping. For their safety, you should not sleep with them. They may be suffocated, you know. It can happen, and it has been known to happen. A mother turning side can have her body crushing on the little ones without knowing, especially in deep sleep right after birth.

Angel feels sorry, and immediately apologized. I know I can trust you with all my heart. I guess I am out of control. I would never do this to you again. Mistress seems to be the one feeling sorrier. She is prepared to do any thing for Angel who has gone through so much hardship. In their long chat, Mistress offers the most comforting words possible to Angel, the nurturing mother, who has no one else around but her. Those words can never be as good as from her own mother, as Angel knows subconsciously, but her mother exists only in her imagination.

She recovers from her pain in a few days. It is good for her, because she will soon find herself too busy even to care for herself. She wishes her mother is around, a mother who can give her all the answers.

Do I know what my mother looks like? Trying hard as I can, I cannot remember at all. Was I born in a pig factory, or in a family home? What did I look like when I was young? No doubt I look like my parents, or rather, they look like me. Did my mother have the same trouble I am having? If it in a pig factory, I suppose she would not feel as lonely as I am. I wish they can send me to the pig factory now, together with my babies. I swear I shall make my babies remember me. They will never forget my face. No, I will not allow that.

It is an entirely new experience for her as a mother. Everything she does for the first time seems to go wrong. Trial-and-error is the only way to grope her way forward. Try again and again. The proper way is never found. Each time she does things a little differently. Then she reviews from her experience. It is so frustrating that sometimes she is about to give up. But what can she do? Giving up is not an option, she tells herself.

Mistress tries her best to help with her own human experience. I should get diapers. She asks around. Lady, are you kidding me? I have never heard of piglet diapers. She makes them from cotton cloth. The piglets would squeak as either mother wraps diapers around their little bodies, and they would yank the diapers out with all their might.

It is early summer, not too cold for the piglets to spend daytime in the backyard, together with at least one mother. They would leak anywhere. The flowerbed would be their choice playground to trample on. The backyard garden can look no better than haphazard bomb shelters. There will be no harvesting of tomatoes and beans from the food garden enclosure this year.

How can they manage so well in pet shops with so many more pets? They put them in cage, but this idea has never occurred to Mistress, even without Angel around. There will be no cage in my house.

Instead, there will be playpens, mobile ones on wheels that can be moved from room to room. Accidents do happen. You hold one piglet at a time. You wrap it with a blanket, and it can still leak on you, sometimes right onto your face. You wash your hands with soup all the time. Sometimes you would not even bother using soup. They always demand your immediate attention.

The washing machine is put to the utmost use, as are standby floor mops and buckets. The profession of Mistress is put on hold. New offer of projects must be turned down. Grumble can be heard around the house. Angel complains often, but she has yet to hear that from Mistress. She signs. When can we get rid of them? It would be nice if they can be toilet-trained. How long do we have to wait? That will be the day.

At night, they will spend time in the garden shed, together with Angel. This is when Mistress can have a well-earned rest, but not Angel. Coaxing them to sleep is an impossible task, especially with two around. The night seems so short. There is no chance of Angel having a wink after daybreak. She is suffering from sleep deprivation, but there is no cure.

How do you discipline these naughty little devils? How do you make them listen and remember what you have said? The only recourse is to show them your stern face all the time. The moment you relax or smile is the moment you turn your computer off without tabbing the 'save' key. All will be deleted. It will take a long time to boot up, right from the very beginning.

The piglets are never tired when they are awake. They run around, when she cannot afford to steal a nap. It would be too risky. Who knows what they will be up to next? They jump, and they can hurt themselves. Their bodies can be thrown against the wall, or a table leg. She shouts to them all the time, but her warning can never last long. They like to push against her body when they want to sleep. It feels nice, even when pushing keeps her from sleeping well. It is so warm and cosy bundling together.

She is into breastfeeding them. Human mothers can install regular hours, say every four hours or so, but not her. Is it because piglet is different from human baby by nature? She does not know. Worse, feeding is never continuous. They come and go as they please. It makes her feel like an ever-ready feeding machine. Drop a coin and press the slot. This machine cannot be allowed not to satisfy your demand. Kick if the machine is asleep. The machine is so tired that often it cannot be bothered with what is happening.

Isn't it nice that I have two? They like to fool around with each other rather than get close to me. It is good that I can be left alone rather than engaging in those silly games. My only chance to get a closer look is when they are asleep. Perhaps I can be closer to my baby if I only have one. Banish the thought. I should have four, if they all survive, but it is not that bad. At least I have two now.

Autumn is coming. The piglets, though still babies, are growing up fast. They are learning new tricks everyday. The two mothers slowly come to realize that there will be no let-ups. The minute to think that they can get used to the hassle is also the minute they will have to face a new trick. Playing catching up is so challenging, yet so frustrating. When will it ever end?

Is it time for them to be weaned? Wouldn't it be nice if they can be toilet-trained? Are they ready for both? If so, it can only be done one at a time. Which should come first? These questions are on the mind of both mothers' active planning, but the answers are soon found to be unnecessary.

CHAPTER 3 ANIMAL KINGDOM

She has a vision. The family are out for a picnic, all four of them. The piglets are not in the picture. The town park lies with the new forest on one side, next to the river. On a clear day, you can see the town nestling in the valley beyond. It is birthday for Mistress. The cake is about to be cut, but the candles have to be blown out first. A knife is taken from the basket. Master is receiving instruction from Mistress, who by this time is pregnant for the second time.

"How do I cut it?"

"You can cut it into four pieces. There are only four of us. You can finish what Big Sister cannot finish, if you really want to. Oh! You better not. Remember what the doctor says about your cholesterol level?"

"It is a blunt knife. I shall have to press it hard into the cake."

He cuts deep. The cut is so deep that it reaches all the way down into the blanket and the grass below. The four slices move continually away silently from one another, slowly and steadily. She and Big Sister are behind one slice, in turn with the forest behind them. Soon she can only see the sun in the distant horizon. She is not frightened. Neither is Big Sister. It is all so peaceful, like a ride on a magic carpet.

She and Big Sister trek in a leisurely pace on the forest floor. There are birds humming and hopping on tree branches above, and scattered wild flowers on either side of the trek. They reach the bottom of a steep mountain, and climbing up becomes more and more difficult. There must be some invisible hand helping them, as they are totally unprepared. Clambering down to the valley below, they find a T-junction. Not knowing where to go, they stop for a break. Two boys, a cat and a dog, come up.

"Excuse me. Can you please tell us where this road leads to?"

"Going ahead, the road will lead to Pig-land. Behind you is Human-land. That is where you come from, I believe."

"Where does this third leg lead to?"

"This is Main Street of our Animal Kingdom. You may like to have a tour if you are free. We can be your guide. We have time."

The two girls have a brief discussion. Why not? We have all the time in our life. We are wandering travellers waiting to explore whatever comes our way. This is an interesting proposition that we have no reason to refuse.

"My name is Angel. She is my Big Sister, Mary Lou."
"Welcome to our Animal Kingdom. I am Catherine. Call me Cat if you like. This doggy friend of mine here is Wolfgang. It is nice meeting you."
"We feel the same way too. Thank you. We would have been lost without you."

"This is a kingdom? Who is the king?"
"Not any more. We have none since the last lion king's death. All that is left is a governing council."
"What does it do?"
"Not much. Councillors settle disputes. They meet part-time, serving like a jury with experience."
"Do you come to them when you have fight and quarrel?"
"We would rather not, if we can settle those between ourselves."
"Do you have fights often?"
"Almost every day. We fight for everything."

"It is bad."

"Why do you think so? There is nothing wrong with fighting."

"It cannot be bad for the strong. What if you are weak and end up losing."

"You will always end up winning or losing. That is what fights are."

"But it will be so unequal between the weak and the strong."

"They are unequal. You know that. You cannot make them equal."

"But the winner will always be on top."

"Of course he will be, but he cannot be sure next time."

"Would you help the weak by any means?"

"Why should we? It is up to him to help himself. By the way, fighting will help him in the process. They say practice makes perfect. I say practice will bring improvement and win."

"Fighting between the weak and the strong is not fair."

"It is not fair if there is oppression, like the strong trying to stay on top forever."

Angel is troubled by the thought that they will never have peace. It is anarchy. Then she thinks of another term to describe it. It is dynamic peace, a peace with a life of its own. How interesting! Anarchy can be good.

Wolfgang joins in at this point.

"One of these days, I may want to become a councillor too. It is no big deal."

"How do you become one?"

"I can offer myself for the job. They are thinking of holding elections. Some say it is bad because that will bring in politics and politicians. What do you think?"

Master once said politics is a necessary evil in democracy, but Angel does want to go further on that.

"Election is good. It is fair that both the weak and the strong have votes."

Angel takes a glance on Main Street. There is settlement on both sides. She can see animals in groups, each tending their own business. It is similar but different from the main street that she is used to. There are no buildings and shops, but she can see colonies of settlement separated by thickets, tree trunks, and open space. She can feel peace in the air. There is no hustle and bustle as in human streets. Here you can relax.

"Is the boundary of these colonies fixed?"

"As long as it remains fixed while it lasts. The boundary separates herds of the same kind. No animal has a claim to a particular area. The land belongs to all."

"Would the same herds fight to protect their own territory?"

"Almost all the time, but I cannot see anything wrong with that."

"Will it ever stop?"

"What for? It is natural, don't you think? Herds contract and expand. Old ones disperse, and new ones are born. If a herd cannot hold on, it should move on."

Angel ponders. This is what they would call natural justice, or the law of the jungle, as humans would say. This is evolutionary law. It would be difficult to argue against it.

In the distance, she can see a large lake or pond, with various animals scattered around. Some are drinking, and some are having fun in the water.

"That is our watering hole. It never dries."

"It looks interesting. Shall we go down and take a look? I am thirsty."

"Let me showing you the way. You must be careful not to go through the wet part of the marsh. It is dangerous. You can get bogged down by the deceptive soft mud. You will not be able to get out, and that will be the end of you."

Death is not what I want, Angel says to herself. Not yet, anyway. Catherine seems to have read her thought, and does not hesitate to give her an opinion.

"I call that a long sleep, a sleep from which you do not wake up. Not ever."

"Would you believe that you will go to heaven then, or to hell if worse?"

"What is heaven and hell? I do not understand your dialect."

"Do you mean you have no religion?"

"What is that?"

"Never mind. It is just something that some of us believe in. I can see that it is not in your culture."

"We believe in waking up every morning, until it is time not to wake up tomorrow. We live for today."

"I am sure you do, and I cannot agree with you more, but do you not worry about tomorrow?"

"Why should we?"

Angel can see lilies-of-the-valley spreading in front of her, all the way down to the waterfront. It is a beautiful sight. This is idyllic country.

"Wofgang: are you and Cat always good friends?"

"You bet we are. Some say cat and dog can never be friends. I cannot see why not. We two are a good example."

"Is there not any fight or quarrel in between?"

"You bet we have. Yesterday we had an argument. Cat told me to shut my face. I was so angry. I yelled back at her."

"That is right. I made up with Wolfgang early this morning. Our quarrel can never last long."

Angel thinks of herself and Big Sister. Sometimes I have the urge to tell her to shut her face too. In fact, I have done that several times, but she will always be my best friend. I love you, Big Sister. We shall always be on each other's side, whenever the need arises. No one can separate us.

Angel can see young wolverines chasing one another in the distance grass. She wants to ask whether Catherine and Wolfgang is each other's best friend, like her and Big Sister. Would Wolfgang only have a dog as his best friend? She holds back. This question may be too sensitive.

"Wolfgang: do you make very good friends with dogs like you too?"

"You bet I do. Some of us only play with dogs, but I find that so stupid. You make friends with whoever you want to befriend. Why should I bother whether she is a cat or a dog?"

Round the corner, they can see two bull moose locking horns. It is rutting season. The sound of banging heads can be clearly heard. It is a fierce fight. Angel is very concerned that they can kill each other. The likelihood of permanent brain damage cannot be ruled out.

"Shall we stop them?"

"Absolutely not. It can be very dangerous even for us to get near. Besides, they must have a score to settle, which we know nothing about. We should leave them in peace."

Angel shouts in her head. You call this peace? This peace involves killing. It is an oxymoron, right? She can feel blood rushing into her head. Then she calms herself down. This is their peace. Some dynamic peace it is. Try as it may, they can never convince me of any peace with an ongoing battle to hurt each other so ferociously.

The battle is over. One moose is limping away, apparently wounded, probably badly. Angel sighed with relief. None is killed.

"Would the winning moose be punished for killing another, if this is found out by the council?"

"Absolutely not again. Why should he? He has done nothing wrong. Such things happen. He may end up being killed in stead of being the killer."

Angel thinks of murder in human term. Perhaps those humans are right. There can be no murder among animals, because they never plan and scheme to kill one another. Death is an accident, an unintended consequence, and an unfortunate outcome. Death as a phenomenon should be swallowed whole, with no aftertaste. Life and death is but a natural cycle. Dynamic peace can be peace after all.

They bow and lower their heads to lap up water on the shoreline, including Big Sister with her long hair flowing in the surface. When she comes up, the hair covers her face so well that you cannot tell which side her face is on. On one side of their small group of four, there is a bathing elephant herd. One elephant mother is spraying a sprout on a frolicking baby who has yet to control his jelly trunk. On the other side there are gathering zebras forming a fuzzy screen of black and white stripes. There is continuous movement. Some gaps are left wide open. Between gaps there can be seen animal bodies pushing against one another for space. The animals apparently have not yet learnt to line up and space out properly. It is chaos, yet chaos with an underlying order.

The surrounding is worse than any playground with free-roaming kids. It is noisy, with the young and not-so-young kicking up sand at one another, and at perfect strangers. Parents would watch close by with no intension of interfering, and would not say sorry for their kids' bad behaviour. It is a place no human mother would allow their children in.

The water is cloudy or worse, with rotten vegetation in bits and pieces suspended and floating up and down. The pungent smell of animal sweat is everywhere, in the air, in the water, and in every mouthful. If Mistress were around, she would have stopped all from drinking immediately, but she is not, fortunately or unfortunately. Big Sister must have forgotten her mother's warning about cleanliness and health hazards, and so has Angel. The water can even be described as fresh and sweet, if you can ignore the muddy and rotting taste altogether.

Angel notices two rivers: one meandering before flowing into the lake; the other beginning with cataracts and rapids. Marsh can be seen close to the former. She wonders how something that looks so peaceful and tranquil can be so life-threatening. There cannot be a better trap. Why does the council not do something about it?

"Why do you people not get rid of the marsh? It can be easily done, you know. Just dig a channel to drain the excess water. You can build a barrier along the shoreline, and in time you will have recovered from the lake a valuable slice of land for development. Indeed, you do not even have to do anything on that recovered land. The marshy soil is so fertile that vegetation will soon cover it up, to produce excellent food."

"I don't know. Yours may be a good idea. The governing council may like to hear about it."

Immediately Angel regrets what she has said. I must never tell anyone to interfere with nature, unless it is absolutely necessary. What if a few animals get bogged down in the marsh? Inevitably there will be some careless enough or adventurous enough to be killed, but this cannot be a good reason to drain the marsh, which is a wonderful participating part of the ecosystem. She corrects herself.

"No, I am just joking. I think you should try your best to keep the marsh as it is. It is so peaceful and beautiful that it would be such a pity to see it gone."

To cover up her embarrassment, she tries to change the subject.

"Are you afraid to die, like being bogged own in the marsh?"

"I would certain hate to be bogged down. I have seen it before. It is a slow death. The more you struggle, the more it will suck you down. Staying motionless is no rescue. You would die slowly from starvation. Worse still, anyone who tries to help can be sucked away as well."

"What about death by other means?"

"Do you mean like getting old, or getting killed accidentally in a fight? I cannot see anything frightening about that, though I must honestly hope to see another day. To be asleep forever is not that uncomfortable, from what I can see. The only part sad is that my friends and family will miss seeing me, and I seeing them."

Angel cannot decide on what he has said is philosophical or not, but it surely make some sense.

It is getting late. They should get back to the trek soon. However, they are advised that travelling in the dark is not recommended, as there will some steep slopes to climb. No one will be able to help them if they have an accident. Not much is known about the trek ahead. It can be risky in such unknown terrain.

Both Catherine and Wolfgang offer to put them up for the night.

"But it will be too much trouble for you preparing bed for us. Is there a hotel or hostel somewhere nearby?"

"You can choose from many comfortable flat surfaces to lie on. We are not going into our shelter tonight. It is such a glorious night that it would be a waste not to sleep in the open. We are heading to the sandy beach. Would you care to camp with us?"

There is no way the two girls can resist the temptation.

"You can see my shelter from here. It is about three quarters way up the slope, just below the peak there. Wolfgang's shelter is near the bottom. He cannot climb as well as I can. I am living there with my brothers, sisters, and parents. Usually there are only a few of us around, except in a storm, when you can find all of us."

"Do your family own the shelter?"

"Yes, it is our own shelter."

Angel hesitated for one moment, before appreciating Catherine using 'own' as adjective, not verb. Ownership means differently here.

"How long have your family lived in this shelter?"

"As long as Father settled in with Mom, before we were born. I or my brother may leave later to settle elsewhere. If we stay, it will remain in our family. Otherwise it will become vacant and available to whoever wants to move in."

So that is how their 'ownership' can be understood. User is owner. It is that simple. Angel recalls a street scene back in town, when a car parking space is under chain and lock whenever it is vacant. Other cars looking for parking space may circle round and round, but that locked space will remain vacant. It is such a waste. Why can they not made it available to whoever is in need? Suddenly it dawns on her. Not only is animal unequal to human, but one human can be unequal to another as well. This talk of human equality is just that. It is no more than talk.

On reflection, she cannot help pitying such stupidity. In wasting their resources, they are paying a hefty price. They could have been a lot happier, had they been smarter and more fair-minded. Why is it so difficult for them to figure out this point which is so obvious? If Master were around, I would show him how efficient life can be. Look at this watering hole. Can you humans organize it any better? I do not think so.

Perhaps they think they can. They can price the water frontage parcel by parcel. This wide stretch is reserved for a millionaire who may visit a week each year. That narrower stretch is available for first class drinkers. The middle class will have the widest stretch, on a pay-as-you-go basis. Those paupers will have to line up and wait for their turn on a lesser stretch, holding a cheap ticket. People who cannot afford it will have to thirst, or wait for some charity drink. As for us animals, forget it. You are destined for the slaughterhouse anyway. Why can they not give all equal rights, even if everyone is born to be unequal? There is enough water around. You can drink as much as you can, and anytime you want.

Refreshed, they retreat from the lake. Angel takes a last look before turning her head. If my camera is with me, I would take one wide-angled picture of this evening here. I would edit the four of us at the bottom of the picture, and I would like to write our names on the back, in case I forget the names when I look at the picture at old age. Better still, I wish I can do a painting right now. She turns her head, to take one long final look. She wants to remember it, and keep the picture in her head mentally forever. One of these days, with canvas and brush, I am going to have it done for all to see. I would explain the story at the same time as I show the picture.

Angel can feel some pang of hunger. She thinks of the biscuit in the backpack left after lunch. Suddenly she does not feel that hungry. Then the offer comes.

"Would you like to join us for a barbecue dinner? There should be enough food for four."

"Excellent. We certainty would. I am dying for some hot food."

They reach the intended spot on the beach, under a new moon. The barbecue fire is lit. There are mushroom, onion, chilli, potato, and other exotic vegetables. Chunks and pieces of meat lie on the shelf. There is no knowing from which animals these meats can come from.

"Where did you get your meats?"

"We scavenge for them in the forest, as usual."

"Did you not kill or hunt?"

"We seldom do that. What is the point of going through all that trouble if you can scavenge for free?"

"Do you mean that you will always get your food by scavenging unless you have no choice?"

"We dogs and wolves always do that. We descend from a common and sensible ancestor, the Middle Eastern Grey Wolf. Vultures get their food only by scavenging.

Lions sometimes kill for fun and sport. Some killing does not make sense."

"How do most of these animals die?"

"They die of various causes. Some die of old age. Some are killed by accident, or by killers. Some do not recover from wounds. Look at that retreating moose just now. If it does not heal, it will be ready for scavenging."

"Dead meat is not fresh. It may not be fit for eating."

"What do you mean? Newly-killed meat is not fit because it is tough and stringy. It may cause indigestion. Gamey meat should preferably be left to age for a week or so, although sometimes you cannot afford to wait against strong competition. If you wait, the meat will be eaten by others. Fresh meat is only good to eat if from an animal physically disabled such that it has to stay in more or less in the same spot for its whole life."

Angel cannot see any dead animal bodies around in the forest.

"If you scavenge only to get your meat, would there be enough?"

"Remember we are not strictly meat eaters. We eat fruits and leaves too, while keeping plants alive if we can. I don't know whether you call that scavenging or what. We eat roots, and sometimes we kill the plant, but that is alright. It is easier than killing other animals for food. As I have told you, I seldom do that. Occasionally I may chase a rabbit to eat, but that is hard work. It is not worth the effort."

Angel looks at the forest floor. She can understand why it is so clean. They sweep it up for any leftover food. There is no waste. They have no landfill problem in this kingdom. Everything is recycled.

A thought arises in her mind.
"Do you eat your own kind? I mean, if you find a dead dog, would that be your meal or not?"
"I would."
"But it is so gross."
"What is gross?"

Dog eats dog. It sounds so cruel. You think you are sensible enough not to waste good meat, wherever that may come from, but you make me sick. You are uncivilized and barbarous.

Angel has not been eating pork since long ago. She wants to reprimand Wolfgang, in as nice a way as possible.
"It is wrong to eat your own kind."
"I don't see anything wrong if it is good meat, which will be eaten anyway. Why not me, when I am hungry? What is the difference? I can see that you feel strongly on this matter, but you have not given me a reason."

I can give you very good reasons. Angel searches her brain. It is abominable. I can tell you that I would not do it even if I am starving to death, and so should you.

Then she realizes that these reasons cannot be persuasive. They are more like religion or dogma. Years ago attempts were made to persuade the Chinese not to eat dog, just as Chinese should not eat one another alive, as portrayed symbolically in novels on those feudal and not so feudal times. Strong reasons have been presented and rejected based on their culture. The Chinese have a right to refuse, and so should Wolfgang. I should give him due respect, in the same way that he should give me due respect for not eating pork. I may call him cruel, and he may call me stupid, but that is alright as long as we act on our true feelings. On the other hand, why should we annoy each other? It has been such a good evening. Why should I spoil it now?

"By the way, I can tell you that we have no pork here today. I hope you try some of these meats. They are delicious. You are not a vegetarian, are you? My brother is. I can never understand why he should impose such restriction on his diet. It does not make sense to me. I guess he has his own reason. It may be some reason beyond his control, or reason that he may not even be aware of."

She swallows her discomfort at the thought of cannibalistic dog eating dog, though the thought lingers on inside her long afterwards. Her disrespect for Wolfgang gradually fades away as the evening wears on into the starry, starry night.

As they start eating, Catherine and Wolfgang ask about the part of the world where the two girls come from. Do you live in herds? How long do you stay with your family before you are on your own? Do you have many sisters and brothers, or is the family small in size? Do you camp out often in the open? Do you fight among yourselves like we do? Is your lifestyle similar to ours?

What can Angle say? Perhaps she can say: We are from your future. We are time travellers. I have bad news for you. You future will be bleak and miserable. You will be kept as pets. What is that? It is difficult to explain. A pet is like a doll or a toy, except that it is alive, to the extent that it will eat and drink, and move on four feet. A pet will be kept by a pet-owner for fun and entertainment. What is an owner? He is someone who can do whatever he likes to do with you. He can be cruel, or he can be very kind as in my family. When I talk about my family, I do not mean my parents and siblings. I do not know whether I have brother or sister. In fact, I do not know who my parents are. I am adopted by the best human family in the world. All members of the family are humans, like Big Sister. They all look alike except me. Our lives as pets are dictated by humans. Whatever we know is learnt from them. We pets have no history and no memory of the past, and we have no future. You think it is a miserable life? No, it is not that sad really. I am having fun, and I make them happy. What more can I ask for? I do not know. Maybe it is just me. I should be happy, but I am not. I guess it is my own fault.

Angel is thinking of telling them about the slaughterhouse. Some of my kind is not kept as a pet. In fact, most are not. They are kept in a factory for no other purpose than to be eaten. Cats and dogs like you are different from us pigs. You will not be eaten, not where I come from anyway. Why is the difference? I do not know. Let me say you dogs and cats are luckier in this respect. Where I come from, you will all be pets. In other countries, you may also serve as meat.

In the next instance, Angel has made up her mind. Why should I spoil it all by telling such a sad story, almost as if they have done me something so wrong that I must avenge? Why can I not wrap up the night with something more cheerful? She has a brief discussion with Big Sister before making up a story as best as she can see. Big Sister will pretend to be tired, and will keep quiet so that there will be no contradiction.

She begins by describing the human world from what she can see around her today. It is very similar. We have forest, river and lake. We live with our parents. It is called the human world because the majority are human, not pig. We eat more or less the same food as you do. We quarrel, and we fight with each other. We live for today, like you. You want to know about religion, hell, and heaven? Those are our cultural things which some of us do not consider important. My explanation of these complicated things may bore you to death. They may have no relevance to you here. Yes, we are nice to each other, like you. Why should we not? We live to be happy.

There is really not much that she can make up, as she is not in the mood to make up like a novelist. Trying to imagine and describe the best can be painful when one is brought back to Earth by harsh reality. Besides, she never enjoys lying, especially to friends, who are not supposed to cheat each other. It is best to interrupt their curiosity by changing the subject to something more interesting.

"Big Sister and I go to school every day, early in the morning. We cannot say no. It is the law. Our parents will be punished if they do not send us to school. Do you have the law here, punishable by the governing council?"

"No, we do not have to go to school tomorrow. Schooling here is supposed to be for everyone, including parents. Everyone makes his own decision. Why should parents force it on their kid?"

"I don't know, but that is the law."

"Some stupid law! How you can forcibly keep a kid at school, like keeping him in prison, without making him unhappy. Does it work? I mean like force-feeding him to learn. It sounds so unfair to me to keep a kid in prison because of his age. He has done nothing wrong."

At his point, Wolfgang comes in.

"I have never been in school myself, but I have learnt a lot outside school, and I can see nothing wrong with that. I can tell you that I am one of the best howlers in the neighbourhood. One of these days, I may even be the best there ever is. I look at others, I learn the best posture, and I practice. One thing I have not understood though is why howling on top of a hill under full moon can be so much better. I am prepared to enrol in school this summer to understand why. You see, I am not against school education. It is more disciplined, organized, and consistent. Once I am enrolled, I shall attend school every day until I have finished the course, because the interest will be engaging. By the way, would the two of you like to hear me howl? It is a call of the wild, as that London guy has described to us in his novel."

Angel would like to say no, but she would rather not disappoint. After both girls nodded their heads, Wolfgang raised his sight to the sky in its infinity. It is a weird, shrill, and horny sound lasting for a couple of minutes, a sound much better than Angel has anticipated. It cleanses her soul as she is brought into meditation. She does not know whether that sound has any meaning at all. Perhaps it has some spiritual meaning, too complex to be understood. There is no doubt the sound comes from nature, long before speech is invented.

Wolfgang stares at the two girls, to keenly watch their reaction.

"I am sorry. This is not good enough. I could have done better. Next time you should come with me to the hilltop. You can hear echo from the valley below, though you can never be sure whether it is an echo, or whether there is someone howling back. To tell you the truth, I can seldom restrain myself from howling back."

It would have been nice if the night can be stretched for a couple of hours more. They have so much to talk about that none of them wants to stop, but there will be a long and difficult trek ahead for the two girls tomorrow, and they should have enough rest. It has been a long day. As the last voice dies down, they all stare at the star-lit sky. Angel has never seen so many stars before. She remembers once sleeping the night in the family backyard, all by herself. Why is it so different? Is it the beach sand, or is it because Big Sister is sleeping beside her? She does not want to find out. She just wants to savour the moment.

Next morning, she wakes up with the sun in her face. It is so peaceful, but it will not last long. Suddenly an alarm sounds, not from any alarm clock. She must warn them.

"Have you ever thought of your kingdom being invaded from Human-land or from Pig-land? I am not threatening you, but it can happen, you know."

"I have never thought of that. Maybe some in our government have, or may be they have what would be called a contingency plan, but I have never heard of it. Why would they want to invade our kingdom? It does not make sense to me. What can they get from us? Why should they disturb us? We have never disturbed them."

Angel has some possible answers, but she would not say it out. They may have a population explosion problem, and they want to grab your land. More likely, they may do it for greed or vanity. They want to master you and turn you into pets. Worse still, they want to turn you into meat machine because they find you tasty. They can wipe you all out of existence, before you can see one soldier's face. Perhaps your best contingency plan is to surrender before they do anything. Tell them like this: Look, we are all yours. Do what you like, and we will not say one word. Just be lenient with us. The land is yours from this moment on, and we are at your disposal. The contingency plan is never to fight back, but to surrender quietly. Do not think of or ask for any miracle, because there is none, absolutely. Those science fiction tales and movies will never come true. There will be no happy ending. Do not say: let free or die, because life is too precious.

It is a sad thought. I hope it never happens, but I shall not mention it one more time. If these animals are happy living for today, who am I to deprive them the right to do so. I shall always keep you in my mind, and I shall pray for you. May your kingdom last forever! If the invasion does happen, I only hope they can turn it into a nature garden, with you animals kept as exhibits. They should at least have the decency to keep you animals alive, even if as captive in your own land. In the meantime, all you can do is to wait for the day when they can set you free. I am waiting for this day too. This day will come, like the day they set their slaves free.

CHAPTER 4 PIG-LAND

It is a long trek, much more difficult than can have been imagined. Those nature barriers separating the Kingdom from Pig-land consist of cliffs to be climbed, rapids to cross, and slippery mud banks to wade through. It is lucky that there are two of them, helping each other and saying encouraging words. Going alone would be next to impossible. Still, it takes a whole day before they can reach Pig-land, when the sun has already set down for quite some time.

Out of the forest, they reach a house, and they enter through a familiar door.

"It has been a long time. We are about to dine."

"Mom: this is my best friend, Mary Lou."

"Welcome Mary Lou. Come and join us for dinner."

"Where have you been?"

"I have gone to the other side of the snowy mountains."

"Really! It must be very dangerous. I have never known anyone going beyond those mountains. Look at your bruised hands. Are you hurt? We are very worried about you."

"I am alright, except a bit tired."

"A young girl like you should never travel that far alone. Thank God, you are back safely."

"I am not alone, Mom. I have Mary Lou with me."

"I have a thousand questions to ask you, but I suppose you two must be hungry by now. You can tell us all about your trip after dinner."

Twin Little Sister cannot wait. She literally shovels Angel into a room for something very urgent.

"Look at this dress I have bought this afternoon. You think it is nice? It looks nicer on you, Angel. Try it on. Your belly is swollen. Are you pregnant? Do you know who the father is? Who cares! Tell you what, you can have this dress in the meantime. It looks prettier on you than on me. You can return it to me when it no longer fits."

Angel does not want to leave Mary Lou alone for too long. She is fully aware that Mary Lou cannot feel comfortable suddenly in this entirely new and strange surrounding.

Angel finds Mother whispering into her ear afterwards.

"Did you pick her up in the forest? Do her parents know she is with us, or is she an orphan? Whatever happens, she can settle down here as our family pet. She looks nice. There is no pungent smell in her. You can show her the bathroom after dinner, and I shall arrange a temporary quarter for her. I know. She is your best friend. Don't worry. I shall treat her nice."

Father cannot help raising a question.

"Do you know the boy well?"

"Do you mean the father of my pregnancy? Of course I know him well. We do it not by remote control, you know."

"Angel, you must remember to be polite to your father. He means to ask how long you know the boy."

"We have been together for many days during this long trip. He is a wonderful guy, and very handsome too. You will like him."

"Is he your age? Where does he live?"

"He lives on the other side of the forest."

"Is he smart, like you?"

"Of course he is. You know well that I would not suffer long with people having no brain. They make me sick."

"How smart is he?"

"It is difficult to say. In some ways he is smarter, but in other ways I can beat him without question. But you cannot deny that he is very knowledgeable. He is different. You may think you are smart, but there is no question that he is smarter than you. He knows what I want. Daddy, he is my intellectual soul-mate."

He is smarter than me, huh? Have I not heard this before? I know. Daddy has stopped being the smartest guy for some time. Besides, who can beat this halo of freshness worn above the head? It may wear off in time, but I hope it stays on forever. I am glad that you have found a good mate, or male mate to be exact. I shall always wish the best for you, my dear daughter.

Angle recollects her mating experience, and cannot help wondering how so much can happen in one night. Does time stop, or does each minute stretch into an hour, like a sweet dream of a lifetime in a short nap? The soul-searching journey of the two continues, from beginning to end, with agreement and argument on what has been long buried in the heart but never forgotten, as if they are seeking answers to the meaning of life. They talk of Madame Rolland and her husband, the Paris Commune, the Grapes of Wrath, and freedom with all its implications. Mating is an intermission in the talk, when suddenly both subconsciously realize the need to focus in silence. What an intermission it is! Lava is built up steadily and unnoticed inside, until the pressure is so strong that the top is blown out. The volcanic eruption brings wave after wave of earth-shaking tremor, so devastating as to be no less than a dying experience. The climax feels like a victory celebration of national liberation. There is too much energy inside struggling to burst out. The body is so exhausted that it begs for mercy. The head says: Enough. The heart says: No, there must be one more time. Then it starts all over again. Freedom! Angel wants to shout out, but she must hold herself. With the slightest disturbance, it may be gone. She has all the time in her life to shout out later.

Finally the climax subsides. Waken from the trance, they wish the seed of a future generation will be implanted in Angel's body. They can foresee resistance leaders standing behind barricade built with everything thrown in, including the dead bodies of their fallen comrades. The struggle for liberation and for a better world is not just for pig, or for female, but for all.

They departed as soul-mates and like comrades-in-arms, not knowing whether they will meet again. They swear to each other their devotion on committed lofty ideals, preparing to sacrifice at any cost, and never to give up. They will be there, whenever a cop hits a farmhand on the head. They will not leave anyone suffering alone.

Mary Lou at first follows Angel's example by calling Mother. Soon she changes to calling her Mistress. She is not Mary Lou's mother after all, and who knows what the neighbours will say. Best friend or not, a pet is a pet.

But for the concern of Angel, Mary Lou's life would be very miserable indeed, away as she is from all human contact. Why it is so miserable cannot be understood except by Angel with her past experience. Mary Lou feels like a sole survivor from some major disaster. A bird in a cage would have a better time hearing other birds chirping outside, jumping from branch to branch. A small cage for a bird would be more comfortable than a wide open garden for her.

One day Father returns from an overnight hunting trip in the forest, dirty, tired, and excited.

"Look what I have got in the van. We shall be having something exquisite for dinner."

"Do you have a good time, Honey?"

"You bet. I shall cut that up and put it in the big freezer. It will last for weeks."

"Quiet. Mary Lou is inside. We must not let her know."

"Why? It is not against the law. She will know sooner or later."

"Whatever. How do you think she will react seeing this mangled human body? We must try our best to hide it from her. She can be that sensitive. She deserves respect, just like you and me."

"Look what I have got from the forest, Darling. I harvested these manna pods very early this morning, well before sunrise. They still look very fresh. It is high time for you to savour this delicacy again."

"You brought in more last year."

"The quota has been cut again this year. They estimate that the marauding human herd has increased. With the way things are going on, I would not be surprised if they may cut the quota to zero one of these days."

"Why do they put those humans ahead of us?"

"They reckon that the herd will not survive without manna. They would do anything to protect the herd. There are some strong animal rightists in our government. They want to protect the manna-producing flowering ash tree to eternity. You know what, I agree with them too, even though I am far from being an animal rightist. Sorry, but what I mean is that I agree on the need to protect the ash tree, not on those humans having priority over you on manna. On that, I would always put you above those animals, you know."

Though immersed in her videogame, Angel must have overheard her parents' conversation on the human herd being threatened.

"Why can we not leave the forest alone to the herd, so that humans can have as much manna as they like? We can have our own space, and they can have their own in the forest."

Before Father can say anything, Mother counters that the forest is not for human living alone. There are many other animals there too. Some of us pigs also live there. If your father stays bachelor, he could be one of them. It is wrong to segregate exclusive habitation in townships, or whatever you may choose to call them.

Father finds his turn to speak.

"There is enough manna around to be shared by all. If we do not harvest the manna pods, they will rot away and be wasted. Besides, your mother likes them very much. She deserves them more than those humans."

"Whatever happens, Daddy, you must promise me never to threaten their survival. Remember, Daddy: Mary Lou is my best friend."

Father can remember those days when nobody would want to have a human as his best friend. It still does not make sense, even now. But what does he care?

"Not to worry. I shall not. I can tell you that I kind of like them. They are peaceful and intelligent. I know. I have observed them quietly in the forest."

The Sunday morning newspaper headline reads: Comet Earlier Can Reverse Human and Pig. It is an extract from True Science, a science authority.

"Angel, have you read that? It says that if that comet by whatever name had fallen on Earth a million years earlier, humans would have developed ahead of us in the evolutionary ladder. We would be animals roaming in the forest instead. It is truly amazing. But then, you should not believe every word those scientists say. They can be guessing, and their guess can be as good as mine."

"You should believe in science. Of course scientists make better guess than you. In fact, they are more than guessing. Their opinion is based on study, research, and investigation."

"We all know that God has made us in his image. A boulder from outer space is not going to make any difference, however long ago that may happen. You know what the pastor said last Sunday? Comets are God's firework, no less."

"I have heard that too. I was in the church with you last Sunday. He was only speaking symbolically to praise God."

"Whatever he means. We have God's feature. No one can deny that God's feature is the best feature ever anywhere."

"What is your point? Of course human has a different feature."

"We are handsome. They are not."

"Don't you ever say that in front of Mary Lou! Don't you ever say she is ugly, because she is not. You should never hurt a young girl like that."

"I won't. Someone said once: feature makes me. It is true. You can tell a lot about a pig by what he looks like. A stupid pig has a stupid look. That is all. God cannot give the smartest feature to both human and pig. That will cause confusion. He cannot force every human to wear a badge, saying: Do not expect much from me. I am only human."

"I cannot agree with you. I think Mary Lou is very intelligent, more than some of us here."

"True. There are some very stupid pigs around. They are mentally deficient."

"Daddy, you should never call the mentally deficient stupid. They are born like that. You should give them their due respect."

"I do not mean that. I am only referring to those who pretend to be mentally deficient, and those who choose to be mentally deficient. Some of them may want to influence us to be like that. Look at those politicians."

"I maintain that you can be equally intelligent even if with entirely different features. Look at Mary Lou. Her ears may look different, but she can hear as well as any of us. Look at her eyes. She can lip-read as fast and as accurately."

"Imagine yourself being God. You have the smartest possible brain to fit into a compact feature. Try squeezing that brain into a different feature, and it will not work properly. If there is not enough space, wire connections will be broken. If there is too much space, the brain will not feel comfortable, as it is thrown about from side to side. In either case, the brain will be damaged. A creature with a damaged brain will be stupid. It is as simple as that."

"God is almighty. I am sure he can make things equally intelligent, even with different features."

"Do you remember what the Bible says? God created animals from our spare rib, a rib we can spare. He did not explain why, but I can guess. He wants the earth to have some higher order to be in control. If we pigs die out by accident, human as the next in line will take our place. It is a big if. They can wait on forever."

Angel has read about that spare rib in the Bible. She finds Father's theory far fetching, but she cannot find a better explanation. He is an excellent handyman. There is no hope of beating him in handyman terms with which he can apply so cleverly. His theory is always based on superficial common sense. How can you argue against the need to have a stand-by?

Leaving Sunday church service, the family of five can see protest at the front of a newly completed compound, part of the branch office building of the Institution of Architects, or IA. Some demonstrators are trying to prevent a small exiting group from leaving. In the centre is someone Angel and Mary Lou can recognise to have met in the forest. Mary Lou shouts out: Auntie Angelina. They cannot get through the crowd who are cordoned off by the police.

It appears that Angelina is the architect for this IA project. There was praise for her achievement until she is discovered to be human. She is now confronted with placards of 'Get Lost', 'No Human IA', and 'Traitors'. The last is apparently meant for her fellow walkers.

They soon learn more. Angelina is a member of the IA, by virtue of which she can take on architectural project. The law specifies that non-pig cannot be a member, at the same time as it has the 'Don't Ask, Won't tell, and Peace' policy. We shall not ask whether you are non-pig. You do not have to tell us so. The result is sweet peace. What is wrong with that?

It seems that Angelina is a member of some IA committees. She has also been in the annual ball. She walks like a human, talks like a human, and looks like a human. Nobody has ever asked whether she is a pig or not, nor has she ever so identified herself. What has recently happened is that, during a press interview, a non-IA investigative reporter asked her that sensitive question. She could have avoided answering, but whether by slip of tongue or whatever, she answered: Yes, I am human. Trouble has been brewing ever since.

Many blame her for coming out of the closet. She should either identify herself right from the beginning, or she should remain silent for life. We have tolerated her by not asking, and now look what she has done to us? Some sympathize with her. She does not come out of the closet on her own. The closet door was opened by that reporter by asking what we have been forbidden to ask.

The meeting inside has been about whether to kick her out of the IA. In this respect, it appears the law is in a twilight zone. It says non-pig cannot become a member, but is has not said an existing member would be kicked out if she is not a pig. Many argue that this is implicit in the law. She should have abstained from membership application, at the same time as she is not supposed to tell us who she is. The onus is on her, apparently. Some argue not. The policy is meant to allow everyone in as long as she does not tell.

The confusion surrounding this policy centres on what happens if she is asked. Is it then alright for her to tell? Don't tell even if asked has not been specified. Of course IA members in following this policy cannot ask, but that reporter is not an IA member. Should we expand this policy? Don't tell if asked, or you are out. This idea seems good, until someone points out the existence of an Amendment called Freedom of Speech. The IA is not like some secret society. It has no right and no jurisdiction on people answering outside the IA door. Either you lie, or you must say you do not know.

Some want to cancel this policy altogether. If it can be causing so much trouble, we should not have it in the first place. Let them in as long as they are qualified. Yet many members would not feel comfortable sitting next to a non-pig. If he is in, we are out. We threaten to leave en bloc to find a new IPAO, short for Institution of Pig Architects Only.

The problem, of course, does not stop with Angelina's membership and her future as an architect. The newly-completed IA building has suddenly been found by many to be ugly beyond acceptance. The mildest criticism is that it has no pig values, whatever that means. Some can smell human once inside. Meeting there is no better than meeting in a jungle. If it feels like a prison, why we do not turn it into a prison? Some goes as far as to attack it as a disgrace to architecture.

On the way home and long after home, they have unstopped discussion, often coming out at the same time that it can be difficult to tell who has said what. Angel and Little Sister, with the former being more vocal, are on Angelina's side, arguing that she has done nothing wrong. Mary Lou is quieter, being well aware that whatever she says about her auntie will be taken as tinted.

"How can they have this policy? It is so stupid."

"Yesterday a guy tried to enter the lady's washroom. I said: Hey. Do you know what he said? He said if I don't ask, he won't tell, and there will be peace."

"This policy is the best compromise they can think of. It is difficult to please everybody. Politics is the art of the possible."

"In the end, nobody is pleased."

"It is true. If the sum of happiness cannot be above zero, you should target on the lowest sum of unhappiness, which is zero. This is good politics."

"Why do they not make it clear by asking outright? Are you non-pig? Alright, you are in. Alright, you are out."

"Many members feel strongly on non-pig membership. It is easier to shovel the problem under the carpet. Forcing a vote can split the IA in two."

"I can remember the past president's campaign promise to get rid of this Don't Won't policy as soon as he is in power."

"He has promised the implementation of so many things as soon as he is in power. How soon is soon enough? He asked for time because of his full agenda. He has never said whether he would repeal it outright, or whether he would replace it with something."

"That is true. Lat week he said in a press conference that if he is given another term, all his past campaign promises can be fulfilled. Trust me, he says."

Mary Loo has a more urgent concern.

"I wonder what will happen to Auntie Angelina."

"Her IA membership will be suspended pending an investigation. They are thinking of banning her from this village. The worst is that she will have to say goodbye to the profession."

"She has done nothing wrong. She has not lied. What can she do? What would you do if you were her?"

"I'll be damned if I am forced to answer yes or no. Sorry, I don't mean to be rude, but there are ways to avoid that. I can say: No comment. I can also smooth my hair before saying: Do I look piggy or not? You tell me. They cannot blame me. I have not said anything."

"I remember that years ago they have the same policy on homosexuals."

"They say old homosexuals never die. They just fade away."

"I thought they say this about soldiers. Who knows, they can be turning homosexuals and humans into soldiers."

Most of them sympathize with Angelina.

"I think these people are simply making up excuses against human Angelina. How could they like the IA building one minute and hate it the next? It makes no sense."

"They can explain. It is like when you are shown a nondescript painting. Worth one hundred dollars at most, you would say. Then you are shocked by learning that it was done by a well-known grand master long ago.

You take a closer look. What a genius! Look at the IA building in reverse. It is well-designed. Done by human? No wonder I feel so bad. I can find things wrong here, there, and anywhere. This can only be done by an animal, not a pig."

Mother has an idea that will help.

"What Angelina should have done is to dress up like those Muslim women, with a black or crimson cloth covering her from hair to toe. Nobody would know whether she is human or pig."

"What if they still ask her: Are you human?"

"She can say: I don't know anything. I must be modest. I am only female. Ask my husband or brother."

"What if her husband or brother say Yes?"

"Then it is alright. They cannot charge her because she has not said anything. They can accuse her husband for telling the truth, but what does he care?"

Both twins hate this idea. They swear they will rather die than to wear such a cloth trap. Angel goes further, horrifying her mother.

"If they are going to execute me, I would refuse to have anything on that I do not like to wear. I shall stare straight into the face of the world until the last second."

Mother shrinks. This daughter of mine is not going to have an easy life. There is little I can help. I hope she has the support of a partner and good friends around wherever she goes.

"I think the law is an ass. The IA is an ass. The president is an ass too."

"You should be careful criticising those big shots. They can take us to court for defamation until we become bankrupt."

"But that is true, don't you think?"

"Your mother is right. You better call the ass an ass if he agrees first. Why should you annoy him if he wants to pretend?"

Angel does not like the joke. She is in a serious mood.

"What they should do is to keep the first half and repeal the second half of this Don't Won't policy. Don't ask, because anyone can be qualified enough to be an architect. Don't tell? Why not? Is that not against an Amendment called the Freedom of Speech? The IA should be a tent big enough to welcome all sorts, including some pigs who dislike humans, and some humans who dislike pigs."

"Does Freedom of Speech not include the freedom to question? I don't know. It is probably better to cancel this stupid policy altogether."

With Angelina not around, the village quiets down soon afterwards. The IA has not explained how the matter has been settled, except saying in an announcement that the best common interest has been served. No complaint can be heard from Angelina. It is not known whether she is still an IA member. If in Angelina's position, Angel would have fought all the way until there is complete victory. It is not just about herself. It is also about all those who are fighting for self-respect, and the respect deserved for those like them. Then she wavers. This is not a battle. This is war. Would it not be better for Angelina to fight inside the IA, to fight another day? Angel is not yet mellow, but she is moving nearer.

It would not be quiet for long. Election campaign is in the air. Free cookies will be in jars on campaign tables. Each jar will contain cookies made after different things, like health care, social security, and senior benefits. A sign on the table says: Take your pick. You are warned not to swallow the cookie whole, because there is a tiny slip of paper showing the campaigner's smiling face, next to several words: Fulfilled by your vote. It is the time of the season to degrade politics from the 'art of the possible' to 'the art of the believable'. Swallow those cookies at your own risk, but paradise is that close. All you have to do is to believe.

Autumn is coming. Father wants to fix a log cabin for Mary Lou. No one doubts that he will do a good job. Autumn is already in full swing. The job has to be finished before the onslaught of winter. The three girls volunteer to help, at first enthusiastically. Angel remains enthusiastic to the end. Mary Lou is restricted by her difficulty to stand up on two legs for long. She is an animal, more comfortable on four legs than two, like a bear.

There are some heated arguments around on what the cabin should be like. Everyone agrees that since the cabin is for Mary Lou, she should have the final say. Unfortunately, she is not that vocal in this respect. She has never been inside a log cabin before. How does she know what is best for her? Besides, she does not want her comfort to be such a demand as to cause family quarrels. What does she know about problems with building a cabin to last through a winter that she has never been through before?

Angel insists that the cabin must have insulation. Otherwise it will be better to call it a summer storage shed. Even with insulation, heating cannot be overlooked. Heating with oil or electricity becomes the next argument. Ducting for wire connection is a hassle, with the ground soil turning hard. Oil heating is out by majority rule. Flooring is the next argument. Again, more is voted than the bare minimum. Angel wins most of the arguments, making the log cabin almost luxurious. This should not surprise anyone. Sometimes it pays to be stubborn.

The cabin will be for Mary Lou's exclusive use during her stay. No doubt it will be used in other ways if and when she is gone. Angel insists on having a very sturdy and comfortable building. She assumes that the two of them, or three if including Little Sister, may have a good hideaway from the adults, comes winter or summer. She is concerned about Mary Lou freezing in her sleep on cold winter nights. Her parents have to assure her that Mary Lou can always sleep inside the house anytime. The switch for the heating appliance is there to be turned on. There is no need to move natural gas bottles over frozen ground. Electricity is more expensive, but safety always comes first.

The cabin is more than half finished. There is still human flesh left in the freezer, though Mary Lou would never have a taste. It is against the law. Father suggests going to the forest before the onset of winter. Everyone knows that he likes to spend time there, even if all alone. Perhaps it has to do with him being the only male in the house. He usually has good reasons getting away. My buddies want me to join in. We are a hunting team. It is time to harvest manna for you. I need to supplement the family income. It is high time for us to taste gamey meat. Mother seems to believe only in one reason. He wants to get away from her.

This time his suggestion is for the whole family to go together. They have done that last year, and almost every year before that.

Autumn is in full bloom. The truck will be more crowded this time, but nobody seems to care. The girls never stop talking and giggling in the backseat of the truck, while it is relatively quiet in front. The parents can feel time slipping away from their fingers. It is another year. What beautiful scenery, which the girls will not bother much to enjoy. They have many more years ahead of them for that.

They step up to a disused fire watchtower. It is first time for Mary Lou. This should be familiar territory for her, but she has never seen the treetop canopy. It is a rainbow of colours: red, pink, brown, orange, beige, yellow, green, and dark, fighting for attention from all directions. You can almost hear a voice shouting from one spot: Look at me. The next instant, that voice has jumped to another spot. The voice moves too fast to allow you catch your breath. The ever-changing colours weave into one another in all fashions, with no consideration for matching or contrasting. How can it be done? Angel can only imagine thousands of blindfolded weavers doing a giant carpet project at random. But that still cannot be, unless those weaving threads and strings change colour as good as the wind flows.

They stay on the watchtower platform for a while. The parents want to linger on a little bit longer, but the kids are getting impatient. Soon they will be driving on to find no trace of manna or those little green flowers. The season is over. Human herds would be more than half way on their long trek south, leaving other animals occasional shaking and shuffling in the brush.

"You know what I am thinking? Those humans have a better time than us. They have a summer vacation in our forest, and now they are going to have a winter down in the warm south. They sure know how to enjoy themselves."

"I agree. They have all the manna they want without worry about quota and all that. I have to do with that pittance you bring in once a year for me. Did I hear you say our forest? It is not ours. It is theirs."

"You know what I am thinking at this instant. In my next life, I want to be a human for a change."

"I know. You have always enjoyed going to the forest. I bet you will not mind living in the forest all by yourself, all your life. But remember, if you are a human you will be hunted, not a hunter."

"I shall be both, hunting and being hunted. I don't mind. I can play hound-dog one minute, and rabbit the next."

Mother glances at her husband. He has a better life than mine already. Let his next life be even better as a marauding human, but I shall not be his wife. How can I as a housewife keep track without a house? It boggles my mind. The other day I went to a bank. The bank clerk asked me about my profession. I said housewife, and he put a cross in the form. My girlfriend, who has recently given birth for the second time, told me a similar story. This government clerk asked when she would be working again. She told him that she has never worked so hard in her life. He should have asked her when she can be released from being both mother and housewife. The government should raise her salary, not taking advantage by asking her to work for free.

Mother continues to muse on her next life. I do not mind taking on any career as long as it is a job with fixed working hours. Nine to five or nine to six, it does not matter. I would like to have at least two weeks off each year. Oh yes, give me a day or two off each week. My husband grumbles without realizing that he already has it better than God, who only rests on Sunday. My resting hours now will only last as long as the truck is moving. This rare moment, unfortunately, comes only once in a year, and it will end soon when the truck is finally parked. It is a big forest. They can run around and get lost. How can I keep an eye on all three?

The parents stay for a long time in one corner of the platform, while the girls keep on circling from side to side, sometimes in opposite directions. Father is wearing a jersey newly-knit by his wife.

"Does it fit you?"

"It fits very snugly. I feel so warm. Thank you, my darling wife."

"I shall knit one for Mary Lou next."

"Will she be comfortable in a jersey?"

"She must wear something warm in the winter here. We have heating in the house, but she may go to the log cabin that you are building for her, and she may catch a cold on the way. It takes time for the cabin to warm up."

"I see, but she is a funny girl. She would not mind wearing anything, however uncomfortable, as long as she feels it pretty on her. Sometimes she likes to wear as little as possible, or not at all. You can never guess what is on her mind."

"It is true. She wants to show her figure. I have to convince her that her figure will show up better with a jersey on, and that the knitted pattern will enhance her beauty."

Father seems to understand. That is it, then. If I want this human girl to keep warm by wearing something, I have to convince her that she looks prettier that way. It is useless to warn her about catching a cold. I remember having heard of those human women in the desert, who like to be flattered on how pretty they are, at the same time as they would cover themselves up from head to toe, except either in prison or at home. How can they be ashamed with their look, and be proud of it at the same time? Surely they cannot be complex enough to have a guilty conscience of their beauty or ugliness. I guess I can never understand the pea brain of this lowly animal.

Mother has not yet left her thought on knitting.

"It is not easy, you know, knitting for a human. I have never done it. I am afraid I may make a mess, but it has to be done. No such jersey can be bought from the market."

"I am sure you will do a good job."

"I have a problem taking her measurement. She has a queer-shaped udder. It is very sensitive. I put a tape close, and she sways from side to side, as if I am tickling her. How can I measure her?"

"Perhaps you can ask our twins to force up her hands, and hold her steady from behind."

"You hunt and shoot. You have steady hands. You can measure her for me."

"I can, but I would rather not. Young girl like her may not like me to get that close, you know. Besides, my hands would hate to touch those shaky fluffy things."

"I always wonder how a human mother manages when she has more than two babies. There would surely be fierce competition among them."

"I have observed them in the forest. I seldom see a mother with more than one baby. I suppose she does it one at a time."

"Being pregnant is such a painful experience. What a waste time to have one at a time only."

"They are not efficient. Remember, they are of a lower order. They do not work as well as we do. It will take them a long time to evolve, to be like us. Hey, about Mary Lou, I know how to deal with your measuring problem. We can use a scanner on her. All that is required is for her to stand still for one second. I can transcript it for you digitally afterwards. It will be an easy job."

Mother has not finished on the jersey yet.

"I asked her what pattern she wants on the jersey. A girl like her, you know, can be very conscious of fashion, especially when she has Little Sister around."

"What did she say?"

"She said she wants a colourful one, like a rainbow. I asked her to draw it out for me in crayon. She said she does not know how. Can you suggest something?"

Father is about to say: I cannot help you. Shocked by a flash of sunlight, with a hand across his forehead he sees something dazzling. Look at that, behind those pines. There lies a rainbow of colours dominating by a crimson oval in the centre. Nature has knitted a jersey so beautiful that no painting can ever hope to compare. The intricate pattern is beyond belief.

"This is the pattern I would suggest. I am sure Mary Loo will love it. Nobody can say no."

Emulating nature is much easier said than done. Mother smiles calmly, trying to remember as much as she can. The burden is on her to make the attempt.

They get back into the truck. The road has turned into a sandy track. Everyone seems to be caught by the bumpiness. Talking has stopped. It is a rough ride, fortunately not for too long.

The truck stops in front of a fence. Ahead there is very competitive undergrowth. The forest is coming back with a vengeance after some previous punishment. They get off, and soon the girls are going ahead so fast that Mother has to catch her breath playing catch up. Her vacation is over. Father shouts out direction, while she keeps count.

They reach the hunting log cabin. It is larger than the cabin yet to be finished at home. It can accommodate three comfortably for the night, if you describe sleeping on that cabin as comfortable. There is hardly anything inside, except some shelves on the walls with hooks. Above the ground are wooden planks with opening between each. The planks sit on truncated tree trunks. It must be a rough life spending the night there.

Mary Lou opens the latch, to Father's surprise.

"I don't know she can do that. She must have learnt it recently from helping me build the log cabin."

"I told you she is smart, Daddy, but you would not believe me."

Mother is concerned that there is no lock on the door.

"We used to have one, but it was broken by my neighbour who had dropped the key. It has been like this ever since. We reckon it is alright this way. Anybody can come in any time. We do not mind it being used by strangers who may find the need to pass the night. As for animals, I do not think any animal would be smart enough to open the latch. Mary Lou can now, but where can you find an animal as smart as her?"

He is apparently trying to please Angel, but it may also be his true belief. He can see Angel smirking.

They sit down on the platform for a rest and a drink of water. Soon the girls are outside, and the parents have to follow reluctantly. It is stuffy inside, with the smell of rotting wood.

Father is familiar with this part of the forest. He asks Mary Lou whether she remembers having been around. Does she recognise any tree or any particular spot? Mary Lou shakes her head.

"Do you remember where you have left your parents, or when you have been lost? Can you remember being with companions or playmates?"

She shakes her head again, trying so hard to recollect that it hurts. Suddenly she seems to remember someone calling Big Sister. Is that someone calling me? If so, that must be my younger brother or sister. How can it be so confusing!

They stop questioning her. Father knows how easy it is to get lost in the forest. You can go in circles, and you cannot remember the spot that you have been through half an hour ago. Things grow fast. Flowers bloom overnight. Storms clear for a change of scenery. Each season brings along its own creation, and each plant grows or dies in an unpredictable way. It is nature, absolutely beyond your control.

The conversation is now focussed on hunting.

"Why do you hunt, Daddy?"

"Why not? It is a good sport. It keeps me fit. I enjoy it very much. I bring in good meat for all."

"But it is so cruel killing them."

"Not more cruel than animals killing one another in the forest. They suffer more pain that way than being shot by us."

"You may not kill by a single shot. You can wound them instead, and they would suffer."

"I usually close in soon afterwards. If they are wounded, I can finish them off right away. Then I take the dead body home for gamey exotic meat, and I leave no mess. We can call hunting recycling by nature, or whatever you like, but it is neat and sporty, even without that recycling argument."

"What if you have shot a nurturing mother? There will be no one to take care of the babies then?"

"Oh, that. Look, I usually aim at single adults, the big ones. If I accidentally shoot a mother or a baby, I would bandage it and let it go. Does that satisfy you?"

"No. What if the mother is shot dead, but the baby is alive?"

"Then I would take the baby home, and feed it as a house pet, just like we treat your good friend Mary Loo."

"We hunt them. They do not hunt us. It is not fair."

"We are of a higher order. Fox hunts rabbit, and we hunt fox. It is dictated by Mother Nature, who wants to keep the stock strong by asking us to cull the weak and sick, and to keep the size of the stock in check. The herd cannot do it themselves."

"Whatever you may brag about, I still think it is wrong to hunt and kill."

"You can say that to the fox. Does he think it wrong? Can you persuade him not to hunt rabbit? If he says it is not wrong to hunt rabbit, he cannot blame me for hunting him. It will be a double standard."

"But he does it for food. We can avoid doing that. We can survive on grain and vegetables."

"The fox does not always hunt for food. He does it for fun too. I have seen foxes fooling around with their prey. Have you seen a cat playing with a mouse?"

Angel knows she cannot win this argument again. She doubts whether she has ever won an argument against him at all. The most she can get is his silence, which means enough, or over for now. What is it called? We agree to disagree? Leave everything said to be unsaid?

By the time they return to the village, the sky has turned golden. It is nice to drive into the sunset. They say if you chase the sunset fast enough, you will never lose it. It is like the sun playing catch-me-if-you-can with you. Go on. I am just in front of you. You stop, and the sun stops, teasing you. Don't give up. I am just that short distance away.

They are home. Father is already thinking ahead. I must finish that log cabin for Mary Lou soon. There is not a day to waste. Tomorrow I would ask my neighbour to help. I hope that lazy bugger does not give me any stupid excuse.

Snow is flying when the cabin is finished. Mary Lou has never seen snow before. It is the coolest thing ever, cooler than anything she would say 'cool'. It is fluffy and soft, so soft that it would melt the moment you feel it touching your hand. She sticks out her tongue, waiting to catch a flake, and she soon finds one landing on top, weightless and tasting so fresh. She can never suppress the urge to go out into the open when it starts to snow, often with one twin or two. Mistress would warn them about catching cold, but Mary Loo cannot believe how warm it can be. The snowflakes fly about in all directions, up and down as if there is no gravity. Their dancing about must have generated the warmth for all to feel. They are like angels, tiny little ones that want to play amongst themselves, and to play with whoever comes their way. It is her experience of a lifetime.

Her jersey has undergone three alterations. The easiest part to knit is around her waist, which she wants to fit tight to show how slim it is. Knitting the part above the waist is most difficult. Too tight, and she feel uncomfortable; too loose, and she will say it does not fit her shape. Should the jersey go as far as her knees? Mother initially insists that it should go even lower to keep her legs warm, but she wants to show her shapely legs, which she claims to be the prettiest part of her body. Mother knows. She has gone through that before. She can never convince these young girls that it is more important to keep warm than to be pretty. It is not worth catching cold. In the end, a compromise is reached, at some length halfway above the knees. Mother would spend all her spare time knitting to catch up with the approaching winter. It is as if every minute counts. The twin sisters would be assigned to cook dinner and prepare sandwich lunch. Soon the kitchen becomes fully occupied with three girls milling around. It is difficult to say whether the kitchen is messier, or noisier.

The jersey is done five days later than the log cabin, after a final alteration. All agree that it looks pretty on Mary Lou showing her shapely legs, which can also be icy cold, especially after she has gone out to the cabin.

One evening she comes out of the bathroom, wrapped under her waist with a rectangular towel patterned with two sets of concentric polka dot rings, like a surging bull with two red hot eyes on either side. Angel comments that it looks nice, and Mary Loo starts to giggle. What do you think, Little Sister? How about you, Mistress?

She walks to and fro in front of them. Facing the wall, she bends down to show a funny face between her legs. Standing up, she gyrates, round and round, in a clockwise direction. Her supple ass moves back and forth, as if waving to onlookers. Stopping for one short moment, it resumes circling in a counter-clockwise direction, as if teasingly say: Come up here. It is like titillating raindrops splashing off an umbrella. Roused by handclapping, Father's attention is drawn. He cannot look away from the whirlpool of polka dots, the attraction being so strong and soul-freeing. Recalling those fertility rites and witchcraft dancing which can be so tantalizing, he at first tries to resist the temptation to be pulled in. Then he gives up without thinking. His mind touches the edge of the whirlpool. It drops in, and once in it twirls with excitement, going faster and faster. Sucked by a powerful force, it shoots like a salmon for the rapid, aiming at the bulls-eye which welcomes it with a full and warm embrace.

His fantasy is shaken away by another clapping of hands, which draws him also to clap but absentmindedly. Mary Lou turns facing them to make a curtsey. Thank you. Thank you all, and thank you for the boys and girls who do rock and roll, and make my life so sweet. He finds himself confronted by the second bulls-eye. That beautified girl will leave a lasting impression. Feeling still constricted, hot, and wet with dense sticky pearls of sweat in the forehead and elsewhere, he suddenly thinks of his manhood. The girls are fast growing up and leaving soon. Let me catch this moment of excitement. It is a high for him.

Mary Lou gets into the habit of wearing this towel every day before going to bed. It cannot be comfortable, and sometimes it falls to the ground when she moves, but comfort is only of secondary importance. A little bit later, Little Sister, ever fashion conscious and creative, would trim the towel and sew up a body-fitting bell shape to cover from waist to just below her knees, with a tightening belt from the same material. No doubt Little Sister will be a fashion designer one day.

When all appear readily settled down into the winter, they are once more unravelled by what happens to Mary Lou. She is found pregnant. This might have been found earlier if she was in Human-land, but the surprise is welcomed no less. Soon afterwards, the talk in the house would never stay far away from the subject of pregnancy. There are now two of them around.

Mother is a strong advocate on the celebration of expected motherhood and its fulfilment. Nothing can be holier. If not for us mothers, Pig-land will be no more than a part of that expanding forest a hundred years or less down the line. Humans with baby clasping under their bellies would crawl over the roof of this house, fooling around and curiously searching for what we have left behind. They would break into our house, see our group family photos, and one of them would say: Look at these handsome creatures with their wonderful body shapes. I wonder where they are now. It is incredible how they build this huge shelter. I guess there are many more of them here than can be seen in those photos. Another would say: I bet they have fought themselves to extinction. Let us go out to gobble up manna now. This forest is all ours. I suggest we call it Human-land.

Father does not speak too much on a subject which cannot be his forte. Even if he wants to, he is seldom given a chance to join in. Being the only handyman in the house, he knows he will be busy with whatever soon. The work of a lone handyman is never finished.

Mary Lou's jersey seems doomed to be cast away to a hard-to-reach corner of the wardrobe to gather dust, but it is not to be. Though not noticed initially, Mary Lou's slim waist is no more. Mother is the first to mention the problem, before Mary Lou can make any complaint about being uncomfortable. She cannot be without something warm, since she cannot be kept inside the house all the time. A young girl like her will be bored to death, especially with you twins tempting her to be here and there. However, not any of them can foresee Mother's ingenuity when it comes to solving household problems. She is able to take the middle section of the jersey off, without using knife or scissors, expand it, and knit it back into a whole jersey again, all within a day. Soon she has to do it again. She can never tell how far to go with this ever expanding belly, but she seems to enjoy it more each time.

Unlike never before, this is such a busy winter. Mother feels like she has not a moment to catch her breath. Father yearns for his past life in the summer hunting in the forest. It seems so long ago. He is the only man in the house, with two expecting mothers whom he cannot communicate with very well. Perhaps only a man with two pregnant wives would have understood his predicament. But it is not the same. Here he has a helpful hand to talk to in bed, though pillow talk is often not when he can make good suggestions. More often than not, his ideas are turned down as stupid. He guesses that he can never understand them.

Both expectant mothers are not feeling well. It must be those pregnant sickness that make them so irritant and restless, but you can never tell whether they can be serious or not.

"Don't worry, my Angel. Just calm down. It will go away. I know. I have been there before. I can give you some pills, but you should avoid taking them unless you really have to."

"Mother, this is real. I don't want to live anymore."

"Go on. Take these two pills, and drink plenty of water."

"Should you give them to Mary Lou also?"

"I don't know. She is from the jungle. The pills may not be suitable for her. They may cause side reaction. Who knows what risk there can be. Perhaps it is better for her to wait and see what they say in the animal hospital."

"Should we take her there right away?"

"It is closed during weekend. The earliest is Monday. I don't know what we can do in the meantime."

Everyone signs with relief when at last spring seems to be arriving. The sign of spring comes on and off, bringing with it joy and disappointment, and sometimes both. If they can look back, this long winter in reality is not that bad. There are also many moments of joy and cosiness to remember too. One thing that cannot be unsaid is that there is never a moment of loneliness. They are all in it together.

At last, spring cannot be in doubt. The snow has melted away for so long that one can say with some degree of certainty that it will not come again.

One spring day Father invites Angel to go to the forest with him.

"Would you like to release Mary Lou, now that the marauding human herd is back?"

"Why should she go? She is happy with us."

"She can never be truly happy as long as she is away from her herd. She should be with her parents and siblings. You know that."

"But I would be miserable parting from her. We may not see each other again."

"Maybe so, but do you want to see her missing her parents for the rest of her life? I honestly believe it is cruel to keep her away from her parents. Don't you?"

"Can I have Mary Lou with me forever?"

"It is not against the law, but it is not right. We should have such a law. I would definitely advocate that law if I am the chairman or something. I mean if I am the male chairperson. Not that male or female makes any difference, like one of those unisex things. Indeed, it would be law by now if I were Chairperson Mao."

"Mary Lou is happy with me. We do not know whether her parents are still alive. If not, she will be all alone. You may have shot and killed her parents, or else it may have been another hunter like you. This explains why she is with us."

Father shakes his head in silence, as if saying: you cannot blame me.

"Here, she at least has me as her best friend."

"Those humans live in a large herd, with parents, grandparents, aunts, uncles, and so on. They are smart in minor ways. They can outrun me, and they climb trees. They are adaptive to the environment. Even if her parents are not around, her relatives will take care of her. She will be among her brothers, sisters, cousins, or whatever. She will not be alone."

"Are you sure?"

"To keep a herd animal away for too long from the herd is inhumane, as those of us pigs pretending to be humans would say. We would say it is inpigmane. Sorry, I should say inpigpersone. Those feminists—they are ferocious. They will call me a male chauvinist pig, as if accusing Chauvin of being a sexist. They can go on for ever."

"Daddy!"

"I take that back."

"If I release Mary Lou to her family, would you promise me never to shoot her and her babies?"

"I promise."

Together, Father, Angel, and Mary Lou leave for a forest clearing. There they sit down on the grass, as the two girls chat for an hour or so without stopping, as if unaware of what is going to happen next, while Father's repeated calls for action prove to be in vain. Then it is final goodbye. The girls clasped each other so tightly that both are out of breath. "Big Sister," says Angel, as if a long-forgotten treasure has been remembered. "We shall meet soon." Both know deep in the heart that the chance is remote.

Mary Lou is coaxed and cajoled to move on. With her swollen belly, she walks slowly and hesitantly at first. Her pace quickens until she can hear a shout from behind. "Take care. Remember you are pregnant." She hesitates, and she can hear another shout. "Big Sister, I love you." She shouts back: I love you too. She is last seen disappearing into the herd in the distant growth. They must have mingled with her as they move away into the far distance, and can no longer be seen with increasing dusk.

Angel turns to Father with a harsh glance.

"Daddy, I am warning you. If one drop of flood is spilled on Mary Lou, I will never speak to you again."

The look on Father's face is like what he would be in a dentist chair, under partial anaesthesia, with a tooth being extracted.

The vision is over as she finds herself murmuring 'I swear' in the dark. Then the almost impossible reunion happens in the very next instant. Big Sister is heard outside the door, knocking softly.

"May I come in? Your knitted jersey is ready."

Chapter 5 Donutting

Flour mixed with water makes dough. Doughnut or donut in short is round patty baked from dough, with the middle empty. It is shaped like a round nut, but there are few if any round nuts of this size in nature. Donutting is the art and science of making donut. You cannot find the term in dictionary.

Angel starts her life as dough. She grows up into a baked patty. She gives birth to piglets, and they become the centre. They live on the inside now, and she is on the outside, ever guarding them. This is her nuclear family. Taking away the piglets from her is like emptying the centre of the nuclear family. A hole will be left in the middle, and the family is forever distorted. It can no longer be called a nuclear family, because there will be no nucleus. It is more correct to call it a donut family. This is the situation for Angel without her babies. What would be left of her is but a donut, or a donut family. She may look the same as before, but she is definitely not the same, and she will never be the same again. Her old self is gone.

It happens three months after the piglet birth. She wakes up, and the piglets are gone. She searches for them in the usual places, but they are not to be found. She goes berserk, as any mother would have done finding the little ones gone, those little ones who are so helpless and so dependent on their mother. At last, she calms herself down enough to approach Mistress for help and explanation. She cannot hide her exasperation.

"Where are they?"

"They have been taken away."

"In my sleep? Why did you not wait until I wake up?"

"You have slept so well. You need that rest badly."

"It does not matter. How can you take them away without me knowing?"

"I am sorry. I am really sorry, dear. But it would be easier both for you and for them. It would be very painful for you to see them being taken away. It would be very painful for them too. It is better this way."

"But we are not even given a chance to say goodbye."

"I know. As I have said: I am sorry. I could have done you wrong. You remember me telling you a week ago that they have to go, and you have agreed to let them go? They cannot stay here. We do not have enough room, not when they are growing up. This house is small. They need space to roam around and play."

"They can be taken away later. They are only babies."

"I know. Look at me, with this big belly. Big Sister needs a lot of attention. Master will be away on business trip next week. Domestic help is hard to get. Overnight domestic help is expensive, and even harder to get."

Angel knows, of course. It is impossible for Mistress to manage so much in the house. She is expecting, and can faint any minute. Big Sister is still a kid. How can I blame her? It is so ungrateful, and so selfish. She has done all she can. She is right. It is better this way, for all of us, including my piglets.

"Where are they now? I want to see them. Have they been adopted?"

"They must be in the transition station by now. It is a nice place, like an animal hospital in a grand scale. They will gradually get used to living without you. Young kids like them, you know, adapt easily. They will forget you long before you can forget about them. Oh, I am sorry. I am not telling you to forget them. Dear Angel, you will overcome this loss, and I promise you and myself that I shall try my best to help you. It is unfair on you, I know."

"Will they be happily adopted? Will they be separated from each other? They have always been together. They will be lonely living apart."

"That I cannot tell. We'll see. All I say is that families like to adopt one pig at a time, just like us before. Let us hope they will both be adopted by one family."

"I wish I can see the family who is adopting them. If it is not a good family, I shall say no. I can reject, can I not?"

"Of course you can. I would ask them to notify us when the time comes."

Angel can go on and on, but she notices Mistress nearing exhaustion, after all that hustle and bustle. When the Filipino maid arrives, both mothers are already calm enough to take a well-deserved rest, each in her own quarter. Thank God, the Filipino maid is sensitive enough not to ask provocative questions.

For the next few days, Angel is on and off in a state of denial. They would be back tomorrow. This is just a bad dream. The transition centre has found them too young. They do not have vacancy. The transition centre has changed its policy. From now on, only dogs and cats will be accepted. We have found them in the forest. Somehow they have wandered away while I am sleeping. Our next door neighbour has returned them this morning because they do not want to wake us up last night. They are safe and sound. What happy ending can I ask for?

She also fantasizes about a less than happy yet acceptable outcome. They have run away for good. It is known that children have run away from home to find their future in the world outside. When they are securely established, they will call home. Better still, they will call home after a few days. Don't worry, Mum. We are fine on our way to the amusement park. We shall be back in a few days. Sorry we did not tell you first before we go, but we have a train to catch, and you were so sound asleep that we did not wake you up.

What is important is that they are safe. Besides, children cannot be expected to stay with their parents forever. Eventually they will leave you. It is just a matter of time, whether sooner or later. From this angle, leaving sooner is not such a big deal after all. She sighs with some relief, but the worry does not go away. I wish they are older, she tells herself.

Despair follows. They have been bitten to death by ferocious barking dogs with sharp teeth and dripping saliva. They have been smashed to minced meat by a passing truck. They have been stolen and found eaten as roast suckling pigs. Mistress has not told me so, because she thinks I would go crazy with grief.

She tries to calm herself down by thinking of Mistress, who has gone through so much. It is very unfair to have her handling this problem, especially given the condition she is now in. She has done so much for me, but I have given her nothing but blame. She loves them as much as I do. There is really no choice. The piglets must go. I t is only a matter of sooner or later. She has made the best arrangement. If I were awake, I would have only made things more difficult for her. It is better this way.

Then she questions herself. Am I not much better and luckier than many in the human world already? As a mother and female, I would no doubt be the envy of many women. No one has treated me badly. I am not worse than any female pig. Come to think of it, no one has done me wrong. But this is not the point! What is the point then?

She swears to remain a mother waiting for them to come back, even if forever. At the same time, the two mothers stay on as companions for the rest of their lives, but their companionship will have less talking than before. Angel is responsible, but not to be blamed. Hers is a wandering soul, from nowhere to nowhere. She seems to have lost the meaning of life, or maybe she does not want to live anymore. She pretends to listen to those comforting words from Mistress, and after a long while she can even answer back that she understands. She would say to Mistress, whenever she can, that she would never blame her, and she truly means it, from the bottom of her heart. She would rather blame herself, and this indeed is what she would do when she is alone. She is lost, and she does not want to be found.

Mistress is unhappy too. She has never felt so unhappy in her life. She talks to Master, but he does not seem to appreciate the seriousness of the situation, as he tends to look at it from a more pragmatic angle. Darling, you have done the best you can. I would do the same if I were you. In fact, I think anyone in his right mind would do the same. Given your present situation, this is the most sensible thing to do. Angel would overcome her loss. Give her time. I shall help you comfort her and make her understand. Mistress hesitates. The less said the better. We cannot risk opening up this fresh wound which must be allowed to heal with time.

Alone, she reviews several times on what has been done. Perhaps she should not have taken their advice. Angel should be the one to decide on when, even if not on how. The centre has promised her that it will always act in the best interest of the piglets when choosing who to adopt them, but that promise is no more than persuasion and intention, not commitment. The worst thing is that they have no obligation to inform us who the adopting families are. This translates clearly as that they will most likely not. They have to protect the interest of those families too. We have to trust them. How can you ask a mother to place blind trust on someone who will remain forever quiet? It is a cruel world.

If Mistress is allowed to pick up only one thing to regret for the rest of her life, this must be it. She feels the debt she owes Angel can never be repaid.

Angel has a dream, a dream so real that sometimes she cannot tell which is which. In that dream, she is wide awake when they come to take the piglets away. She can see two men in a red truck parked on the driveway. Come on. We don't have all day. We do not have lunch yet. We are already late for the next assignment. She is pleading with Mistress. Can you ask them to come again tomorrow? I promise I shall let go of them easily. I won't utter a word tomorrow. It is my fault. I shall apologize to them. I shall explain, and solemnly make my promise. You do not have to say a word to these men. How about half a day? We can tell them to come back this evening. How about an hour, or even half an hour? They can wait. We can serve them lunch here. They have to eat anyway.

Angel takes a glance at the two men. They are apparently getting impatient. She can see them grumbling. They talk to each other in a somewhat foreign dialect which is difficult to lip-read. One of them appears to say something sounding like 'rose' and 'yummy'. Has Mistress told them that my babies like to munch on the rose bush? Dirty little rascals, they are. They always bring so much work for you, as if you are not busy enough already. These men now appear morose, almost threatening. They want action right now, or else?

Five minutes, and that is all I want. Let me take one close look, one final look before you take them away. Let me give them a big hug, each on the face. It will not last for more than a minute. I am sorry I have delayed you, and I mean it. No, I will not wake them up. I would do it very lightly. I know. It will be a lot of trouble for you guys if they are disturbed now.

As Angel extends her hand very slowly to touch those rosy cheeks, she tries her best to remember their looks. Never shall I forget them, she tells herself. It is a moment frozen in time, and that moment will never melt. It is a moment that will stay with her for the rest of her life, a moment that she is prepared to give everything for. Yet it is only a short moment, too short for her, as if it can ever be long enough.

She wakes up from her dream. Her mouth is so dry that she has to rush into the washroom. She does not realize it at first, but she is now transformed into a donut. She may look no different than before. She is solid from the outside, so solid that there is no way for anyone to enter. She is tough, and the toughness clearly shows. If you stay with her long enough, you can sense that hole inside her, however hard she may try to hide it from you. She hides it because she does not want you to touch her soul. She wants to keep the pain to herself. The pain is hers alone, not to be shared with anyone. The pain is too precious, and priceless to her.

It is not an easy job comforting her. You should only do it if you are prepared to suffer the consequence. You can pat her on the shoulder, or you can gently massage her neck. Do not say you understand, because you don't. Do not ask her to forget it. Do not tell her it is all over now. You can keep her company, but if she wants to be alone, you must leave quietly. This is the minimum respect you should have for her. When you are with her, the best you can do is to show that you care. When you are not, the best you can do is to pray for her.

Chapter 6 Healing

Does time heal? Good question, deserving a good answer, but there can be more than one answer, and the answer can be more complicated than a simplistic yes or no. Time is no more than an outsider in the healing process. You want to be healed, but you may not be healed. You do not want to be healed, and yet the healing process may go on by itself. One thing is sure, though. Time does help.

The hole in the donut may never be solid again, but it helps to fill it in, rather than to leave a vacuum. Warm air in the hole will help sooth the pain away somewhat. This air can be empty thought, daydreaming, preferably good fantasy, or even denial of reality. Thus it can be cruel to ask the donut to face it. Take that air away, and the hole will feel so painful as to be unbearable.

As the days go by, Angel begins injecting little by little warm air into her hole. She tries to warm herself by being rational and realistic. What is done is done. I must face it. I should not ask too many questions and in turn demanding too many answers. I should not blame myself and others. I have done all I could have done.

She begins to withdraw from talking to Mistress about her sad loss. Such talk always ends up with Mistress feeling regret. This is not what she wants, after all that Mistress has done for her. She convinces herself that Mistress is blameless, and she would go as far to believe that she would do the same, had she been Mistress. Gradually she learns to appear nonchalant. I have forgotten my babies already. It has happened so long ago. I have a meaningful life ahead. Why should I bother about the past? Deep in her heart, she knows Mistress cannot be fooled, but this is a good way to get away from the subject. Her noticeable hardening almost frightens Mistress. From now on, there will a shelf between the two of them. It would prove to be futile trying to drive a crack through. If indeed the shelf cracks, it will be very painful for all concerned indeed.

She desperately needs someone other than Mistress to share her painful experience. It should be someone who has gone through that similar experience. Where can she find her? She discovers that there are such people around organized in what is called the support group, with members calling themselves abductee mothers. There is such a group in town, holding regular monthly meetings. She can attend the meeting without being a member, but she does not want to be there physically, being well aware that she may most likely be the only pig around in the group. To be the centre of attraction is not what she desires.

She finds an internet chat room group. She only listens at first, but soon she cannot suppress the urge to join in. It is an informal place where you do not have to identify yourself. Before beginning her story, she must first replace the e-prompter by the voice actuator. The surge of feelings in her brain would be difficult to manage. Mistress must not be brought into the picture.

"My babies have been taken away during my sleep."

"They have been abducted. Have you reported to the police?"

"No. My mother knew beforehand. Her husband was away. I believe she has made the arrangement."

"Really? Why did she do that? She has no right."

"The house is not big enough. She has warned me in advance."

"I believe you said babies. How many of them are there?"

"They are twins."

"Are you disabled?"

"No, I am not. I can handle them all by myself."

"What kind of mother have you got? Does she hate you?"

"No, we love each other very much."

"I don't believe it. Is she crazy?"

"She is not, but she has to do it for my own good."

"Come on. She cannot do this to you. You must report her to police. They may charge her for aiding and abetting the crime, but the important thing is that they will cross-examine her, to find out where the babies are now."

"All we know is that my babies were taken to a transition centre. We have given up all legal rights to question the centre on how they would deal with them. There will be absolutely no visiting. We could have withdrawn the decision, but it is too late now. They have the right not to reveal who has adopted my babies."

There is some hesitation on the other end. Then Angel can detect trembling anger in the voice.

"How can you believe in all that transition centre shit? If I were you, I would tell that fraudulent mother of yours to go to hell, at the same time as I would disown her right away. Don't you love your babies at all?"

"I do, but what I can I do? They are gone, and I know they will never be back."

"You can never trust anyone completely, even if she is your mother. They say there is a price for everything. When the pay is sufficient, there will be transaction.

Has your mother been in tight financial straits? Is there a visible change in her lifestyle? I do not know about your mother. I have nothing against her. But I feel you should be warned. Do my questions ring a bell? In any case, it is good strategy for you to apply pressure on her. Don't be naïve. Everybody does things for a reason. Some will sell her body and soul for a price, let alone their own grandchildren's. By the way, your babies, how old are they?"

"They are newly-born, yet to be weaned. I have not named them yet."

"Listen, you must report to the police right away."

Angel thanks the advice. She knows it is useless. Her case is not of abduction. It is done in good will, not with malicious intent. It is not against the law for an owner to give away baby pets. Even if it is, she will never report Mistress to the police.

Solace from the chat room is soon exhausted. It is not that she cannot find sympathy and support, but her case is so rare that she can never expect full appreciation of her feelings. Some correspondents even advise that it is her fault to have overslept, and that she does not deserve sympathy if she cares more for her mother than being a mother. Once she asked a correspondent, absentmindedly, what would it be if your abducted children were pigs like mine? She receives an angry response. Hey, this is no joke. Don't you ever try to insult my lost kid! She would always remember not to ask the same question again. Some accuse her mother as a pig, and she would say no immediately. Mistress is never a pig, literally and metaphorically. My mother no doubt is. I hope my mother is as good as Mistress.

Through the chat room, she discovers that there are organized groups, the most radical of which is the Mothers Liberation Front, with the slogan of 'Death to the Swine; Victory to the MLF'. What has the swine got do with it? We are declaring war against him or her, the meanest creature on earth.

Angel does not feel good. What has us swine got to do with it? The meanest creature on earth: is she referring to the abductor or the swine? She restrains herself. This is not a good time to clarify. Swine is no more than a slang to describe the worst. If there is pig-speak, 'swine' may be replaced by 'human', with the same unconcern.

Would she like to be a comrade? Her husband or boyfriend can also join in, as associate comrades. The MLF would make them beg for mercy, as Mistress has said earlier under a different circumstance which Angel cannot remember, but she can sense the same seal and dedication.

She hesitates to join the MLF, though there is no doubt she is on the side of these human mothers. Perhaps they should broaden the front to all women, by calling it the WLF. FLF is even better, to include all females. There should be some BLF for the bullied, and ALF for all animals. I can join one or more of them. Victory to them, but Death to…is a bit much. I do not want anyone to die. I just want them to disappear without a trace. Then we can read about them calmly in history books.

On the other end is WAIL, standing for Women Awestruck In Limbo. It is a silent group meeting to pray at the beginning of the day on the first of each month. It appeals to everyone to take part even if he or she cannot come to the meeting.

MAAD stands for Mothers Against Abduction. Its inexplicable slogan is Lest We Forget, which she finds uncomfortable. Forget about what? Forget to be mad, or forget our lost ones? You do not have to remind me, because I can never get them out of my mind, however hard I may try. The society solicits donation to help mothers in need, whether physically, financially, or mentally, including counselling. Rehabilitation help to returned abductees is also available, though usually a minor demand on the society's resources.

WWEEP is short for Women Waiting and Enduring Endless Pain. This group does not seek donations. This is a group that she would join to share and listen to others' painful experience. Actually she seldom shares her own experience which is apparently difficult for others to understand. The group has a permanent address to facilitate mothers who do not want to weep alone, as well as for those abductees not knowing where their mothers can be found.

CRY stands for Craving for You, with the slogan: Cry No More, which does not seem to make sense. Perhaps its intention is to ask you to cry no more because it is enough for today. Give yourself some breathing space. The group has a permanent website showing the faces of all the abducted, with dates. You can delete the face if you have a happy reunion. Otherwise the face will stay on for twenty-five years. If you suspect that you have been abducted, you can simulate your timed look on the computer for percentage matching. If it is 95% or more, you would be connected with your mother for initial confirmation of other details before reunion.

Angel likes this group. She consults Mistress, whom she trusts above anyone else.

"Should I send my babies' photos to the website?"

"I would think not. Your babies are not abducted as are the rest of them in this website. It will be unfair to their pet-owners if someone accuse them of stealing or abduction. In turn, they may take justifiable legal action against us."

"I am not accusing anyone. I just want to see my babies."

"I want to see them too. The meeting must be arranged by the transition centre, as soon as the pet-owners agree to meet us."

"What if they disagree?"

"Then there is nothing we can do."

"But I am the mother. Nobody can stop me seeing my babies."

"They have the right to do so. Rules and conditions have been made between the transit centre and the pet-owners, and between the centre and us."

For the first time in her life, Angel finds herself and Mistress disagreeing. Why did Mistress take their side in stead of mine? She carries her annoyance into bed, and she sleeps with that annoyance until the next morning, when it becomes clear. Mistress is only trying to instil reasoning on two heads against what both hearts want so much. This is not a matter of winning or losing, as the heart can only win by Angel going mad. Still, Angel wishes Mistress could have been more subtle and weaker in her argument. Tell me lies. Tell me sweet little lies. Help me escape from reality, if only for a little while.

Mistress is about to contact the transition centre. Suddenly she sees a problem.

"If we see your babies, they will remember you as their mother. What if they want to follow you home? What if they refuse to stay with their pet-owners?"

"I shall order them to stay behind. I am paying them a visit, that's all."

"You can force them, but they will be unhappy, and this can spell trouble for the pet-owners."

Mistress is right. In so doing, I shall be disturbing my babies. They may be having a good time now, like when I first came into this family. I was young then. I had many new things to learn. Soon my mother was out of my mind. What if she appeared suddenly then? Would I be better off or worse off?

Soon both she and Mistress decide not to approach the transit centre. Actually the decision is hers for Mistress to agree on. Why should she suppress her visiting desire which has become so strong and so tormenting, for the sake of possibly making her babies unhappy? Why should her babies always come first? You mothers should know. It takes a mother to understand a mother.

Thus ends her thought of seeing the piglets again. It is not true. The thought will never go away. They might meet accidentally on the street. Would she rush forward to hug them, or would she hide in a corner to steal a lasting peek? That is a distant possibility, too overwhelming to think about.

Gradually she comes to realize that her case is not that unique. There must be many animals like her, in the past, present and future. Such things have happened since hundreds of years ago. It is systemic in the relationship between human and animal. Human will always regard this cruelty as natural, and animal will always accept the reality in the end, though both may be victimized. Look at Mistress. She suffers as much as I do. We are on the same side.

If this is not cruelty, what is cruelty? When will it end, if there is ever an ending? What can I do to bring about this ending, or to shorten its coming? The questions keep circling in her mind, until she thinks she has found the authority in a position to answer.

"Hello. This is the Society against Cruelty to Animals. To report a case, please press one. To ask for help, please press two. For general enquiry, please press three. To speak to a representative, please hold."

"Good morning. How may I help you? Please hang up and call again later if you are not ready. We are currently experiencing a busy wave of calls."

Angel could have said: No, you cannot help me. I am not seeking help. But the call is on, and it would be impolite to hang up. Besides, she is alone in the house. Big Sister is in day care. Mistress is in hospital. Master has not yet been back. Her babies have gone, for good. This is not a good morning, not for me anyway. This home has changed, within such a short time, from a madhouse to an art gallery. The silence can almost be deafening.

"Is it cruelty to take kids away from their parents?"

"This is a society for animals. Are you sure you have the right number?"

"I am referring to newly-born animals separated from their mother."

"I suppose you are referring to the pet owner. Does she give up the pet babies voluntarily, or are they stolen?"

So your first thought is on the pet owner. First thought or second thought, it does not matter. I shall explain more clearly.

"What about the animal mother?"

"Who know what an animal is thinking? Has she shown any visible pain?"

So you do not know. I can tell you how painful it can be. But then, you may not agree with me, because it is not visible like being cut by a knife.

"I can assure you. It is very painful indeed."

"Listen. I am not an animal psychologist. I do not deal with these things."

You don't, eh? Never mind. How can you know what an animal is thinking?

"Assuming it is very painful to that mother, would you consider that cruelty? If so, how would you deal with it?"

"Yours is a hypothetical question. It is not against the law to separate animal mother from baby. Stealing an animal is theft, a common crime. Theft of an underage human is more serious. It is called abduction. Forceful removal of an adult human is kidnapping. Kidnap applies only to adult, not to kid or piglet. Napping a kid is not kidnap. Animal, like a piece of meat, can only be stolen, in which case it will be up to the owner to take action. I agree it is confusing, but this is legal-speak. All these have nothing to do with cruelty, unless there is cruelty in the process. Have I made myself clear, or do you want me to refer you to our legal department?"

"No thanks. I just want to know."

"We do not make the law, but we do have a strong influence on law affecting animals. We always welcome your suggestion."

"One last question: would it constitute cruelty if an animal is painfully hurt?"

"We are concerned with physical and visible pain, and extreme discomfort. Animals cramped into cages too tight for them would be considered cruelty. They have the right to space and fresh air too, you know. How they feel themselves is outside our jurisdiction. It is their reaction that counts. For example, if you give them a hard push, and they are hurt when they lurch forward, you would be held responsible."

"What if a truck full of pigs suddenly brakes such that pig bodies are thrown and pressed against one another, resulting in them painfully hurt?"

"That is an accident. It is never cruelty to be painfully hurt in accident. Put it this way, in legal term as far as I can understand. Cruelty can only result from malicious intent, including self-evident negligence which cannot be defended. If the law required a pet to wear seat belt, and the pet-owner does not put it on, then he can be cruel. If there is no such law, we cannot apply the term on him."

"Thank You."

The Society is right, of course. Seat belt is legally required for human only. Go ahead, if you want to put a seat belt on your pet. It is your choice, but you cannot enforce it on another pet owner. Come to think of it, the law is very clear. A child forcefully taken from a human mother is a crime, but not so for a pig mother. The law is not concerned about whether the two mothers would feel differently, because feeling is personal and emotional. The law cannot, and will never, define how you feel to be acceptable or not.

Human can be murdered, but animal is never murdered. That is right. Animal and human are treated differently. Human only knows how humans feel. They do not know whether animal can distinguish between killing and murder.

A dog biting a human can be punished by what can be equivalent to a death sentence, by destruction or termination of life. A man killing a dog will receive a much less severe punishment, or even no punishment. Look, the law is made by human, to be biased in human favour. Imagine law made by pig. Would it not favour pig too?

The law is against human hitting human, but not against dog biting dog. What is wrong with that? We settle our own disputes, and we do not make law to tell animal how to settle theirs. We lawmakers are already too busy. It is none of our business. Better to leave them to have their own natural law of the jungle, which says that might is right. Or else the biting dog may say sorry and apologize to the bitten. Who knows?

What if pet owners are involved? I suppose it depends a lot on whether your pet is biting or being bitten. If a pet owner suffers any damage in this connection, he can always sue for damage in the usual way. If his pet is hurt, the owner will be responsible to take care of it. If his pet is causing trouble, the owner may punish it with his own rule of conduct. Case closed.

Angel cannot argue with these arguments, even if she is a legal expert. She notes that, years ago, white man treated black man like animal. It is easy to distinguish between the black and the white, as between human and animal. Now the black and the white are treated equally, even if it is still easy as before to distinguish between the two. She hopes that, in some distant future, animal will be elevated to the same status as the black.

Yet she still feels something wrong somewhere, even with the acceptance of there being inequality between human and animal. What is it? She searches for an answer in vain. Suddenly, out of the blue, the answer emerges: it is a matter of respect. Humans are carnivorous. Hunting and fishing can surely be justified. Killing is acceptable recycling in nature. The beginning of disrespect, started long ago with the practice of domesticating wild animals roaming in herds, can also be justified on the demand for food to sustain human survival and multiplication. Domesticated animals have since lost their ability to survive on their own. Our miserable life has no purpose than to provide meat or pet. Can you not allow us to roam in the wild before you eat our meat? Can you keep e-pets which can be programmed to be more real than me, so that I can be allowed to live with my own kind? We do not mind if you fleece us to keep warm, but do you still have to kill us in order to wear our skin, when easier options are available to you now? Think about that please.

She can also find more blatant disrespect. Wild animals are kept for display in cages and zoos. They are made to run in races and to play tricks in aquariums, all for the sake of human entertainment. It is not that she is against entertaining human, but that she can find so much cruelty in the process. The brave lion is whipped into submission, and wild horses are corralled. They used to have their own as slaves, but not anymore. Is it because of the cruelty on slave having no freedom? They should think about us next. It is our turn.

Let me reflect on me being a pet. I am a herd animal. I should live with my herd, but I am isolated from any of my kind, from my parents, sisters, and so on. I have been totally stopped from communicating with them. I learn everything from human, and that is all I can pass on, if given a chance. I am no more than a plaything, and my kind in the pig factory are no more than pork machines. We have never been given due respect.

I am not disputing that you may find it essential to keep us for various purposes, such as study, research, education, and entertainment. We can tolerate that, if you can exercise some degree of minimum respect. Do not imprison us in cages for zoo display. Give us open space, even if highly restricted. Do not separate forcefully mothers from babies. Allow parents to bring up their young. Do not separate husbands from wives. Such cruel separation is rampant in animal breeding centres for pet and for meat, though much less frequently now in zoo and safari park. Do not restrict us from mating or giving birth. These are, after all, no more than natural rights of being alive. These rights cannot be taken away even if you are way superior above us. You should have the decency to appreciate that. It is immoral of you to behave otherwise.

She has thought about approaching a moralist on this matter of respect, but it is difficult to find such a person. She decides to dodge the issue of morality. Instead, she wants to think more about a better future for her own kind. What future do we pigs have, given the present options of being either pet or pork, with the latter in the vast majority? She is able to find the help of a biologist.

"They will not survive in the wild. They are domesticated."

"Can you un-domesticate them?"

"There are various issues involved. Introducing a non-existent species to the wild will upset the current natural balance, affecting both plants and other animals in the food chain. To take an example, pig herds may affect butterfly migration routes. We must be very careful in this respect on what implication and consequence will follow."

"Suppose it has been decided to release pigs into the wild. How long will it take?"

"I cannot see why pigs cannot be released eventually. They are, after all, wild before our domestication long ago. We do have programmes to return wounded wild animals and endangered species, but returning domesticated animals to the wild is more complicated. We have to train them and teach them the necessary survival skill."

"How long will it take from beginning to end?"

"We can apply knowledge on wild boar and warthog as reference. I dare say that if we start a programme now, the third and fourth generation can be trained for controlled gradual release."

Trained for controlled release? You have to train us on what we have learnt ourselves long ago? We have lost our way because of your imposed domestication, and we have to rely on you to find a way out now. It does not sound good, but never mind. What matters is that it is as good as it gets.

Like Moses pleading with the pharaoh after escaping from the palace, she would like to plead with the biologist and his kind: Let my people go. Leave us alone to wander forty years in the wilderness. You can even continue to hunt us, every now and then. We would appreciate your kindness, we would remain friends with you, and we shall never engage in any war against you.

Chapter 7 E-meeting

E-meeting is a meeting in every sense of the word. The only difference between e-meeting and conventional meeting is that you do not have to be there personally, together in the same place facing each other. It is an inexpensive advancement of communication brought by technological innovation.

Angel has noticed that a lot of cruelty to animals arises from the human quest for taste. Sure, she has taste buds herself, but she is not obsessed with them. She has experienced food poisoning before, to learn that bad taste in food can be an indication of food not suitable to eat. Yet she cannot understand why food taste is such a big deal to them. Why do they go into so much trouble for what appears to be a side issue to satisfy hunger? There must be a reason.

She seeks the help of the internet search engine, but the answer is not to be found. There is a programme called: Ask the Expert. She forwards the question: Why is taste so important? It seems taste is talked about in everything: the way they dress, the house they live in, the job they take, the jokes they make, and even the way they speak to one another. There is even a class of experts called designers whose life is devoted to nothing else. Like magicians, these people modify things to be much tastier than before, and such modification is usually accepted blindly by others to be in good taste. Taste can almost be like a religion, or a conviction to be sold.

But her concern is focussed on taste in food, or rather, taste in meat. She has not heard of food taste designers, but she would not be surprised if they do exist. To be more precise, her core concern is whether the pursuit of food taste can justify more killing, cruelty, and suffering?

It is her exceptionally good fortune that she is able to engage an expert in this field. The professor is literally an expert among experts on food taste. He has invited her to an e-meeting in his study-workshop.

"Yes. It is that important. Food taste is worth dying for."
"Even to be killed to satisfy that pursuit called taste?"

The professor hesitates for a moment, as if the wording confuses him. But he is not one to mince words.

"Indeed. Life is not worth living without taste. You eat not just to satisfy your hunger, but more for the joy of tasting. Focussing on taste is healthy. If you focus on food alone, it will make a pig of yourself."

Angel cannot understand what he mans. How can I make a pig of myself? Does he mean that I would eat like a pig? What is wrong with that?

"Even if cruelty is involved in the pursuit for taste?"

"You know what. Cruelty is a topic of my strong interest. I have been invited to give such a talk to the Board of the Society against Cruelty to Animals recently. I am against cruelty to animals unless absolutely necessary. To answer your question: Cruelty can be justified if there is no other avenue to attain the specific taste goal. This is what can be called the moral boundary of cruelty."

"Is there cruelty in slaughterhouse and in animal factory?"

"It is not cruelty as long as breeding and slaughtering are necessary to produce the targeted objective. We should kill as painlessly and as quickly as possible."

"How about hunting?"

"Whether hunting is cruel or not is a matter of personal opinion. It all depends on how you feel about hunting as a sport necessary for the fulfilment of living."

"Can we justify imposing additional pain on animal to improve meat taste, like eating it alive?"

"We can, depending on the strength of that taste justification. Taste and pain are correlated. The interface is more complex than most people think. If an animal feels pain, the taste in its meat may be adversely affected, but not necessarily in that order. One part of his body meat may be more affected than another. There are even exceptions where pain will stimulate a meat part to improve its taste. It is very complex."

"Is it a trend to eat animals alive?"

"The trend was started by pre-history barbarians believing that raw meat will enhance their prowess. It is a superstition, of course, but this superstition has never died down, even today. Many of us eat raw food for their freshness. Salad, for example, is taken raw because freshness makes it healthier. Vitamin C would vanish when cooked, as you would know."

"How about raw fish and raw meat?"

"Since before 2010, needles have been placed in the brain to keep fish alive but brain-dead for extended periods. The fish's still beating heart pumps blood out of its body while dying without knowing. Tender slivers are carved off for the discriminating and mouth-watering diner. The kaimin katsugyo technique places needles in the brain to induce a sort of coma. Chefs can carve out a nice steak from a carefully selected steer that is in a twilight state between life and death, to serve with some freshly baked blood sausage or chopped liver from the same steer."

"A brain in coma means not even the brain is dead. Twilight state between life and death: I suppose it means brain-dead."

"All these are technicalities. I have another meeting coming, but I can give you another half hour."

Half an hour with the professor can be worth weeks doing your own research. Nobody in his right mind can refuse this rare opportunity. The professor brings her away from the desk to the middle of the room.

It is a chicken suspended in mid air. It appears alive. Angel can see it breathing.

"Look. This is a brain-dead chicken. The meat will taste much better than if it is physically dead. If you have sharp taste buds, you may have no hesitation paying more for the meat which is as fresh as alive. How much more will depend on your budget line constraining indifference curves, as my friend in economics would say."

"It has no feathers on."

"We are into breeding chicken just like that. Future chicken will be without feathers throughout its lives. We should have done this long ago."

"Would a chicken not be a chicken without feathers?"

"You can ask the same questions about egg in your refrigerator. Does it have a shell? No, because shell is useless. You cannot eat it, and you will have more garbage. Besides, an unshelled egg would weigh 50% less. The saving in handling and transportation cost is substantial."

"Chicken without feathers look so gross."

"No more gross than an unclothed woman. We call that sexual appeal."

"Chicken may feel differently. Would a hen with no feathers appeal to a rooster?"

"Probably not, but animal is of a lower order than human. A female animal is only appealing to a male when she is ready to reproduce. Otherwise mating makes no sense to them. Whether a hen has feathers or not makes no difference."

"Can we leave the chicken's feather on? They may be useless, but at the same time they have done no harm."

"Because feathers on chicken will divert its attention to grow meat, at the same time as they obstruct implanting. Scientifically, we can predict featherless chicken will be the case in future, through evolution. But why wait, when we can speed it up through our selective breeding programmes."

"What are these selective programmes like?"

"We select only the best roosters to mate with hens, so they can produce good eggs for consumption and for the next generation. We separate males and females to avoid undesirable mating. In the old days we used to let those selected roosters roam free, but now we use artificial insemination to produce better result. This also serves to reduce cross-infection and make them stay healthy. As a well-known example, an ox is never allowed to impregnate a cow directly. I can assure you that we do a neat job."

It means the cow will remain virgin, from birth to slaughter. How do they get her milk? No problem. Virgin can be induced to produce milk by ingestible or injected stimulating agents. It is claimed to be organic milk, though they would never mention that it is from a virgin cow. This is the first time that Angel is brought to know what some humans would not know. She wonders whether the same arrangement can possibly apply to a human virgin.

"As well, we implant sensors on various parts of the animal body to monitor meat growth, and stimulators to induce better growth, in the wings and legs, for example. We have recently been successful in body colour enhancement. The upcoming trend is pink in meat, beige in skin, and charcoal grey in bone. Colour can also be ordered in advance for part or whole body display in feasts, to replace less real painting or dyeing."

"But is not direct mating in their instinct?"

"Animal instinct constitutes major hurdles to be overcome in the advancement of civilisation. We would be still in Stone Age if we let such instinct run wild. There is nowadays no animal mating except in the wild, or occasionally in pets. The former is beyond our control. The latter should be better replaced by selective insemination. It is that much more hygienic and effective. Animal rightists may argue against that."

At last, she can understand why they have virgin birth all along. It is so neat and so trouble free for the animal concerned. Why they do not practice what they preach on themselves? Surely it must be within their power to keep man and woman away from direct mating? Can it be something out of their control? An ox can have his sexual desire satisfied by a simulated dummy cow, but what about his girlfriend who will later be giving virgin birth? I am sorry, but you have to abstain. Remember that we are doing this for your own good, and you should be grateful.

To visualize featherless chicken, mating without contact, and human eating from brain-dead animals makes Angel sick enough that she wants to throw out. For a moment, her digitalized voice shakes and stutters. The professor is not sure whether this is a security warning on computer viral attack, but her voice soon steadies.

"Take a look. Can you see me poking this brain-dead chicken? See how it twitches. This is just muscular reaction. There is no transmission of sensory signals. It feels no pain."

"Last time we experimented with a pig. The result is very interesting. I am working on a paper. I can let you have a copy if you like, after the paper has been published."

"Thanks but no thanks. I am not educated enough to read academic papers."

"Can taste justify waste in meat?"

"Yes it can. Taste can justify anything. Waste is no exception."

"Is there any waste in meat that can be reduced?"

"On the production end: No. Even leftover bones are ground into fertiliser. On the consumption end, wastage is rampant. In our metropolis alone, tonnes of good food are wasted. People obsessed with freshness throw away a lot. Up to ten per cent of food in high cuisine is for display only."

"Why should people throw away good edible food just because it is not fresh?"

"Well, it is a free world. If they can afford it, they will replace stale food to satisfy their taste bud."

"Free world indeed," said Angel to herself. It must be a free world where you would be indifferent to what is not in your interest. Those animals, providing your replacement meat with their dead bodies, are not that free after all.

"We feed these animals with grain. Do we not eat the grain ourselves?"

"We do, but meat tastes better. From grain to meat, we get one-sixth of the weight."

Angel is aghast. They feed five times less by going into this food chain, with animal inserted in between grain and human. No wonder starving is reported in the news. It is unbelievable. They can get rid of starvation by a minor change of diet. All that is required is a marginal switch from meat to vegetable. They will not do it because starvation is justified by taste, or marginal taste to be exact. When will they ever learn?

"Is it not a waste to reduce the quantity of food, from grain to meat, by five-sixths?"

"It is not. Nothing is turned into junk. Taste justifies the reduction. The waste produced by farm animal excretion, including methane and carbon dioxide, is beyond our control. Substantial recovery of these wasteful by-products is costly and not justified environmentally."

Angel's mind swirls around. These humans are intelligent, perhaps more intelligent than for their own good. To them, justification is not much more than a matter of personal discretion. You cannot argue against what they should like or not. Hence you can never argue on what should be justified. They invent a reason to convince you, and in turn they themselves are convinced. It may also be the other way round. They need a reason, which is invented to convince themselves in the first place. Is there anyone to wake them up? God would be in the best position to do so. If there is indeed a God, he should know how serious the problem is, and he would have intervened long ago.

Such thought on Angel's mind, though one-sided, is not unexpected given what she has learnt before and after the e-meeting. She is now in danger of digging a hole to fall into. The world has to be saved. She is probably the only one aware of the urgency. What can she do, or rather, what must she do now?

Angel returns home from the e-meeting, flabber-gasted. It has been an exhaustive discovery trip, a trip that has confirmed her worst fears. I must warn them. Give them a wake-up call. It is time to realize their mistake. Come back before it is too late. The least they can do is to drop this monstrous infatuation with taste.

Not long after the e-meeting, she has the chance to see written on one side of a temple hall: 'Drop your slaughter knife; Become a Buddha instantly.' It seems like a vast exaggeration, until she recalls St Paul in the Bible, suddenly converted from a serious prosecutor of Christians to spreading gospel in the old world. The abruptness of the change to an entirely opposite direction is beyond belief yet real, if St Paul's story is believed. Suddenly you have found yourself to be sinful all along, you drop the knife, and you become Buddha. St Paul is believed to be the first pope of the Christian Church. With no disrespect, Pope can be taken as the equivalent of attaining the status of Buddha.

There is also written on the other side of the wall: 'Hell is not emptied; I swear never to become Buddha.' It must be the aspiration of some sublime being, way above what she is. The vow to empty hell alone should be half way there. The attempt, whether successful or not, should make the whole way. Why would he refuse to become Buddha while emptying hell? There is only one answer. He is setting a high bar on himself. This bar is so high that he should know there is little chance of it being reached, but he does not care. This could be his way to push himself harder.

She is humbled. The most I can do is to make hell less crowded. I do not have to swear because I know I shall never be nearly qualified enough to become Buddha, but this should not stop me from helping him.

She looks up to see written on the beam facing the entrance: 'I do not go to hell; Who goes to hell?' Why should I go to hell, when I have done nothing wrong? But of course you have. How can you think that you deserve less than others to go to hell? Would you not offer yourself to go there to help those suffering in hell? You should not look over your shoulder to see if there is someone else who can go in stead of you.

This thought is too much for her. She tries her best to shake it out of her head. Spare me the mission to get rid of the slaughterhouse, and send someone else please. However, the question keeps revolving and will not go away. If not you, who?

Before agreeing on the mission, she wants to know what it is about. What is hell? Is it the slaughterhouse? Suppose she takes the risk of going there to release the gate, and all those pigs are free, will hell be emptied? No, not necessarily. She thinks of the escaped beast that she met earlier on the street. She wonders what has happened to it afterwards, but she already knows the answer.

She has a fantasy. In the middle of an act to free her fellow pigs, she is caught in the slaughterhouse. They put her among other pigs, waiting to be slaughtered. Is she afraid? Does she regret doing it all for nothing? Searching for an answer in her head, she is surprised. No, I still find it worthwhile, and knowing the consequence in advance I would still do it again. In fact, I can foresee well ahead of what is going to happen. I know they will catch me. I come to share it with pigs like me. I want to suffer what they suffer. I do not want to be an exception. I want those pigs to know that they are not alone. I wish they can feel better this way. Even if they do not, this will still be my choice. It is my turn to get inside, to do my share of time before it is over.

She is trapped, at the same time as she closes the trapdoor tightly. It is now not a matter of if, but more a matter of when. Initially, time did not seem to be of the essence, but of course it is, as she later convinces herself. One more day is one day too many.

She wanders into an escape route. I shall plead with them, and they will listen. I shall be successful in persuading them. They would be shocked. They did not know about it until now, and they will deal with the problem immediately, and will thank me for informing them. Suppose it is not that easy. Thy may ask for time to consider. Like me, they have their difficulty too. In the end, we shall reach a compromise. How long will that take? They will solve the problem in the long term, but

I shall not accept that. In the long term, we are all dead. Who said that?

The more she thinks about it, the more hopeless it becomes. Perhaps it is inevitable that she becomes more radical with time. I should shake them up. I should bring shocking action to force them thinking. They would be forced to review what they have been doing all along. It will be a wakeup call with a bang. I can stop them making use of the slaughterhouse. They will get used to not having the house around. They will discover that everyone, including themselves, have become better off. Yes, my justification is rock-solid.

Her life has been infused with meaning. She has a purpose to live on. The more she thinks about it, the more she persuades herself. It has to be done, and it should be done as soon as possible. When she is engaged in thought, she is sometimes seen to be smiling, as if she is remembering something pleasant from long ago.

In the end, she has not done it. It is difficult to say the failure arises from the lack of determination, of courage, or of opportunity. It may also be said that she is fated not to do it. Who knows? What can be said is that she should not blame herself for the failure, nor can anyone else blame her. I hope you readers will agree with me on this point.

CHAPTER 8 REQUIEM

One night it happens. All of a sudden, without any sign, any warning, it happens, not long after Angel is in bed. The pain stops, and the mind becomes crystal clear. She feels like being weightless. Every part of the body is supported to follow her every movement. It is as if there is some artificial intelligence below and around her, understanding, obeying, and following without question whatever move she desires.

There is Grandma Pig below, lean to the extent of being gaunt. It is a big difference from not that long ago, when she was often referred to as a sow. Soul? Her soul has been left behind, and she is now waiting for the train to take her home. She knows there is a novel called Dead Souls by a Nineteenth Century Russian writer, but she has never read it. Grandma Pig has been her nickname for some time, though nobody knows whether her children have given birth. Maybe they address her this way as a matter of respect, or maybe they think she would like to be so addressed. She has accepted this nickname quietly, and in time she is called more Grandma Pig than Angel. Sometimes she is roused to believe that she is a real grandma, and that they have seen her grandchildren. Perhaps one day they will bring her along to see them. It is a comforting thought.

There she is, old Grandma Pig lying below. Angel can see that she is lying very still, hardly making any sound. Her brow is relaxed. The rhythm of her chest heaving up and down is even and gentle. It may be that she in the middle of a sweet dream. There is not the slightest indication of desire to turn sides. No doubt she is having a good sleep. It would be a sin to disturb her.

Angel looks straight ahead. A wide screen is starting the show. Little Angel is seen being carried by a basket into the family room. What a nice little pig, not much bigger than a piglet. She comes as a surprise to the only kid in the family, who at this point in time can only speak baby-talk, a talent beyond the comprehension of anyone in town, except perhaps other baby-talkers. Slowly, little Angel timidly crawls out of the basket, with cover blanket lifted. She is no less surprised than the kid. She sniffs around from the carpet floor to the easy-chair, but she is not about to go near any of these strangers. Suddenly the kid runs forward, as if trying to grap her by the neck. It is a moment that she will never forget. The adults are caught by surprise. With widely open months, they dash in for the rescue. Master is able to hold the kid in the nix of time, shouting "No, no, no." This is the first time in Angel's life history to be saved by a handsome young man from serious physical harm. Those were the days, days of innocence. Why do they not last for ever?

In such a warm family, her timidity is soon gone. Everyone is so nice to everyone else, except perhaps the family kid who can sometimes play rough. It may be just as well that Angel can settle in so fast, since Mistress is soon found to be not that free any more. The kid is now graduated to be called Big Sister, ahead of the second birth.

For the first time, all five of them camp in the city park. Big Sister tries to hitch a ride on Angel. With baby in a basket, the two adults laugh loudly as they see the two girls roll down the grassy slope.

"Angel must be having the sharpest nose in town. Don't worry, Honey. She is not about to crush any worm because she can smell and avoid it as she rolls. Come to think of it, it may be a good idea to take her along to the wine shop. She can tell me which bottle is a better buy."

Before his wife can answer, Big Sister jams in.

"Daddy, you should say Angel has the sharpest nose in the whole wide world."

"You are right. Perhaps I should take her to France in my next trip. She can dig truffles there to bring back home. We can even sell the truffles and make plenty of money. What do you think, Honey?"

"Dream on."

"Bring me along too, Dad. We will have many truffles. We can eat them day and night. Angel will be the champion and win many cups."

"Drink your milk."

"Can I drink it later, from the cup that Angel will win?"

"Drink up and you will grow to be big and strong like Daddy."

"You can win one cup for me, one cup for Daddy, one cup for Mammy, and one cup for yourself."

"What about Little Brother?"

"No cup for him. He is clumsy. He will fall in and not be able to crawl out."

Angel closes her eyes, but the smile does not go away. The screen is now on Little Brother attending day care. He comes back with songs taught in school, and he sings them to himself and to everyone who bothers to listen. Sometimes he even sings them in the wrong order, and sometimes he jumbles them up. Does he know what the songs are about? You bet he does. He is often very serious in his expression. The sun is a big round circle shaped by his tiny little hands. Stars twinkle between fingers for a few times. Rain is falling from above his head. He is straddling Angel now.

"Angie, you are my bess fan, my bess fan in the hole way wall."

"But is Jason not your best friend? You talk about him all the time."

"You know what Sister Rose said this morning? She said: JJ, come here. We did not understand at first, but she said: Yes, you two J's."

"Jason is also your best friend?"

"My second best fan."

"You should say next best, not second best. Second best means it is not good enough."

"I love you Mom. You are my third bess, you and Dad."

"How about Big Sister?"

"Sometimes fan, sometimes not. She is not like Jason. She is too big for me, and she makes me do things."

Angel cannot help giggling at the serious expression on the screen. I bet I shall always be his bess fan in that wall. I shall be a fan to cool him off under the hot sun, when we play hide-and-seek near the hole way through that wall. Hey, kids, come on in. I have made toad-in-the-wall, your favourite. How nice it is to have Little Brother around! He can be that serious that you should be careful messing with him, bess fan or not. He can hit you hard, and he can stop talking and playing with you for days. But he has a soft heart. If you pretend to be sad and miserable, he will always come back to comfort you soon. He may even give you a warning, apparently learnt from Mistress. "Don't do it again, or else …" But as soon as you make a promise, he will forget about the warning, until the next time. He may force you for a free ride, and he can be made to say please. Piggyback on, before I change my mind. This donkey cannot wait all day. It is so hot here in the desert. I must go for a drink in the water hole. Queue up here. I shall be back.

"I wish I can hug those rosy cheeks one more time." To her disappointment, Little Brother does not jump out of screen. Instead, he is now seen to be shouting 'Stupid Fool' at Big Sister. Angel is awe-stuck in the middle, not knowing what to do, and looking somewhat upset. Looking back, Angel cannot understand what there was to be upset about. Bring me back there, and upset me one more time.

Big Sister does not want to go to school.
"He bullies me. Everyone knows he is Teacher's Pet."
"Did you tell Teacher?"
"I did not steal his pencil. He is a liar, but Teacher would not believe me."
"If you have not done anything wrong, there is more reason for you to go to school. Show them you are not a

coward. Look them in the eye, and say No to the accusation, because you have nothing to hide."

"They still think I am lying. Can you go with me to school tomorrow?"

"I shall talk to Teacher. You are a strong girl. You can take care of yourself, and you are not afraid if you have done nothing wrong, right?"

"I am? Of course I am. I hate them."

"You must not say that. Teacher must have a reason not to believe you. He can be wrong. Remember what I have told you. Adults can be wrong too. Have you been wrong? Would I hate you? No."

"Alright, I shall forgive that bully, but I shall never play with him again."

"You know what. If Teacher thinks you are not good enough, you try to be more than good enough. Show him you can be better than his Pet."

"I will do that, Mom. I will beat that son of a sour pickle, and I will show Teacher he is wrong about me."

Mother smiles with satisfaction. This is sweet soothing revenge, what exactly I want to hear from you, my sugar plum. Keep it up. I shall back you up all the way, and I shall defend you with my life.

"Is there anything else I can do for you, Young Lady?"

"Why do I have to go to school when Angel can stay home? Why can't we go to school together?"

Mother thinks of herself as a teacher. I would make sure no one will be seen as my pet. I would have no hesitation resolving student dispute, but it would be wrong to take side. To force shaking hands between reluctant opponents is humbug, like playing God in self-glorification as peacemaker. My job is not about the conversion of rebels, whose existence is necessary to keep the student body vibrant rather than docile. My duty, first of all, must be to help weak and less sociable students than to have a good time with smart high achievers. Those isolated and bullied, being so desperate as to want to die, may have no one but me to befriend in the school world. I would never grade by a preconceived bell curve, so that the last five per cent are considered junk. Education is not a race against the defeated and lost, against time, and even against oneself. Education can be helped by comparison, but never by force-feeding.

She remembers that, once upon a time, she had tried to bribe them with her weekly allowance and lunch money in order to be in the gang. Not enough? I have more in my piggybank. She was laughed at in humiliation. She wishes that Big Sister is stronger, more like Angel. The Bible says: Blessed are the tongue-tied and the humble. As for Big Sister's suggestion to have Angel in school: Why not? Why have I never thought of that? The three of us will go tomorrow morning.

Mother has a meeting with Teacher.

"Did you find her using or playing with the pencil?"

"No, but the pencil was found in her drawer."

"Could it have been an honest mistake? She is absent-minded."

"She cannot explain why it should be there."

"Is it possible that someone has put it there? The drawer has no lock."

"It is possible, but unlikely."

"Don't you think you should give her the benefit of the doubt?"

"I receive report like this every day. I cannot afford to spend time investigating. This is no big deal in school."

"It may not be a big deal to you, but it is to her. Imagine you leave your car unlocked for five minutes, and the police find cocaine inside. How would you feel if you were found guilty?"

"I see what you mean. I have not taken any action against her except a warning."

"But she will be permanently hurt by the warning if she has not done it, because the warning is targeted on her alone. Like everybody else, she deserves the benefit of the doubt. May I suggest that you explain to her further that she is presumed innocent, not presumed guilty. You and I can understand this point, but she does not. She is only a kid. She will take your warning as a pardoning sentence."

"I shall think about that."

"I would insist that you do it as a matter of urgency, not just because she is my daughter. I strongly believe this is what education is about."

The headmaster is adamant that Angel cannot be enrolled.

"I am very sorry, but we can only have kids in the classroom, not pigs."

"Look: Angel here is a kid, like what you are having now. Does your regulation say that a pig cannot be a kid?"

"No, but it says we cannot allow pets in."

"But she will not be a pet. She will study like any other kids."

"If we allow her in, kids will not be able to focus attention on the teacher. They will fool around with her instead. It will be chaos."

"I can assure you that she will be a good kid. She will not cause any disturbance. She will work hard. Furthermore, she is keen to learn, much better than my daughter here. She may even help to discipline my daughter and the rest of the class. You cannot find a better teaching assistant."

"The answer is no."

"What is the difference between her and other kids? Tell me."

"Well, can she speak?"

"Not directly, but she can talk through the use of this voice actuator which I have brought along."

"That is the difference. She cannot speak. If you really want to enrol her, I would suggest you try one of those schools for the deaf and dumb. I can give you the list."

Apparently Mistress cannot prevail. She must thinks of other options.

"If you cannot allow her into the classroom, there is no reason why she cannot study in the school library by herself. I can assure you that she will be very quiet. She can do without the voice actuator. She cannot be worse than any other student. She will not be making any disturbing noise. I can guarantee you that."

"Our regulation says you cannot bring a pet into the school library."

"But she is not brought over. She comes on her own. I cannot see any reason why you can deny her this learning opportunity? You are dedicated to education, right? How can you abdicate your mission, when it is not even against your own school regulation?"

"I have to check whether 'bringing a pet' can be equivalent to 'a pet bringing itself' as alleged by you. I can raise this matter in the next school board meeting."

"She will bring herself into the library as a student, not as a pet. Look at it this way. The moment she enters your library, I shall deny her being my pet. She cannot be a pet without a pet-owner, can she? She is a pig, but no one can say a pig must be a pet. She is non-human, but I do not believe that term is in your regulation."

"Let me think about it. This would be a precedent-setting case."

"If the matter is discussed at a school board meeting, I would like to be invited to attend as a parent to present and argue for the case. I sincerely hope you can sympathize with the situation I am in. My husband is away, I am pregnant, and I have several tight deadlines to catch in my ongoing architectural projects."

The headmaster looks at her deeply. I know. These mothers are going to fight you to the bitter end when they think you are hurting their children. I have been there before. There will be bruising casualties, including me. Unless I spare her now, she is not going to spare me at the board meeting, not by any chance. Is this worth it? Can I afford to waste my time? Think.

Being a genuine believer in his mission, he concedes with grace. In his head, he also concedes that there can be little room for improvement in her arguing performance in the presentation of a strong challenge without causing annoyance. Do not be fooled by the seemingly humble pleading for sympathy. There is a wall of steel behind it. It is like someone offering you a toast. Declining may have the glass of wine pouring over your head. If he knows Mistress can be so quiet in her home office all day, he would wonder how she can maintain the gift of the gab.

Extracting concession from a school headmaster is no easy matter, as most parents would know. He can talk you out of an idea at the meeting, often only for you to discover after the meeting that you have never agreed. It is a hard-won fight for Mistress. No doubt she can be a high performance headmistress in her own right, if given the chance.

In stead of sending Angel to some dumb and deaf school, which may well prove unsuccessful, she has Angel going to school almost every day with her own daughter. They then separate ways, one to classroom and another to library. It is an arrangement that she finds most satisfying. She can have the morning to herself, enjoying peacefully the practice of her profession at home.

Angel would stay in the library the whole morning and early afternoon. On the first floor, she can see Big Sister playing with friends in the school yard. Often they wave at each other. Big Sister shouts at her. Come down and have fun with us. She can only whisper: I love you, while the librarian is staring. Big Sister cannot lip-read, but somehow seems to understand what she is saying. Sometimes she becomes so bored in the school library that she can hardly restraint the urge to join Big Sister in the school yard, but she know that, unlike other library visitors, she cannot afford to take that risk. Mistress has fought so hard for her. It would be foolhardy to spoil it all by some sudden impulse. As time goes by, she finds it easier to exercise self-discipline. It is a dull life, never meant to be so for one her age, but it is also very rewarding, as she will find out later.

Both girls would be picked up after school. At home, Angel listens most of the time to Big Sister about what is happening in class. Angel has not much to tell. Big Sister apparently is not keen thinking out Angel's questions, to the extent that Angel becomes a self-absorbed girl. Her discussion with Mistress is slowly reduced to allow Mistress focussing more attention on her own girl. This self-absorption becomes a lifelong habit. She thinks all the time, as she is doing now while watching the screen.

She feels her tits being pulled, and she can see in the screen that it is feeding time. Hey, don't pull so hard. It hurts. It is painful, yet so sweet. The sensation is out of this world. I bet a male pig will never appreciate how we mothers feel. However hard I may try to describe it to him, he will never understand. As she gently presses her tits, she cannot help speaking to herself: How lucky I am being a mother. God has been so nice to us. It is much more than compensation for the pain. I shall never trade this for anything else in the world. I wonder whether human mothers can feel the same pain and sweetness. If they have ways to avoid the pain, can they still have the sweetness? If so, will the sweetness be different? Maybe they can even intensify it with some sensation agitator fitted with an adjustable knob. They should never be underestimated. If they can control anything, they will. It is their Murphy's Law. I wonder who this smartass Murphy is like. Why not have Angel's Law which says that all pigs go to heaven?

Dump screen, can you get me an agitator? On second thought: No thanks. I shall not allow some human gadget to pollute what is holy to me. I shall keep this sensation all to my self, and I shall not share it with anyone, not even Mistress.

The screen shows the only time when the seven of them are out together: four human, three pigs. Mistress is strongly against it.

"At most I can do is to control my two kids. What happens to the pigs is not my concern. It is up to you if you want to bring them out. Don't bother asking me to help if they are lost."

Master devises a cloth fence from some old camp poles and metal rods to keep the piglets in. In conjunction, an unbreakable commitment is made that only piglets must be solidly in, and kids solidly out. No buts, no ifs, or we all drive home right away. Can Angel, the mother, be allowed in? No way.

"It is all right," Angel mumbles to herself without looking at the screen. She is now in a thoughtful mood. The things they have done for me and for my piglets are truly amazing. They may have done more for their own kids, but what does it matter? They are great. I mean: they are really great. I should always remind myself to be grateful. What have I done for them? I have been nothing but a burden all along, but especially now. They should send me to the slaughterhouse. Yes, they should just do that. I should tell them I am not afraid to die there with my own kind.

The screen is now showing the beginning of the e-meeting with the professor at his study-workshop. Her disinterest and discomfort are reflected in the listlessness seen on her face. I wish this screen can fast-forward. Lo and behold, the screen takes the instruction. When Angle next asks for play, the e-meeting is almost over. She can see the professor making her an offer.

"Would you like to consider a career in my profession?"

"No. I am not qualified."

"That problem can be overcome. What matters is your aptitude and potential. There is a strong competition to enter this field. Because of the bright future, many have tried hard to enter unsuccessfully, but I can take you under my wing. Once in, there is practically no chance of you being out of a job. The pay is excellent. You can earn more in a couple of years than say an architect of many years experience."

Angel is tempted by the prospect. She can help the family income. We can move to a bigger house, or even fly executive class once in a while. It is about payback time after all that the family has done for me. In a split second, her mind is made up. No, I shall never take a profession that would make animal brain-dead, not for a million dollars. I am sure Mistress would not approve that, nor would she switch over to that job, even if her pay is immediately doubled.

What if taking up the job means that she can keep the piglets with her? One should never underestimate how degrading a mother can go, when it comes to her kids. Fortunately for her, fate has not tempted her stronger than what the devil has offered to Faust, which would have torn her apart for the rest of her life.

Being of the inquisitive type, she is not discouraged to find out more.

"How do I start?"

"Like every applicant, you have to start at the entrance study level which will be under the charge of one of my former students. If you like, I can arrange for him to see you. Finish that, and I shall accept you as a doctoral candidate directly under me. There are several of them competing for my time at the moment, and more are queuing up to be under me. But don't worry. You will be under me as soon as you are ready."

"Shall I be studying pain arising from the taste need?"

"It is your choice. The subject, for example, can be on the interface and symbiosis of pain in taste."

"Thank you for meeting me. I have asked much more than necessary."

"It is my pleasure too. I have not come across someone as thoughtful as you are for a long while. You have asked very relevant questions for me to revisit, but I am more concerned about you entering the profession. We need you. Your future contribution would be much welcomed."

"I may not spare the time to undertake the study now."

"That is all right. Choose your timing. You can fast-track or you can go slowly. There is at present a time limit on how long a study must be completed. This is necessary to sieve out non-performing candidates. But you do not have to worry about that. If you have to delay or interrupt your study and research because you are pregnant or want to care for the young, come to me and I shall grant you the necessary extension."

"I do not want to undertake the study as yet. I shall let you know when I do."

"Remember to come to me first when you do. Without my influence, they may reject your application outright. The reward can be enormous, provided you put in a

good effort. As the layman saying goes: No pain; No gain.
"

"Thank you, professor. Why are you so nice to me? I am nobody."

"Listen. I do this not just to please you, but your depth of feeling is rarely found. I would be doing a disservice to let slip your possible contribution to my profession. I am very good at spotting talent."

So he is doing it for himself and for the profession. This thought is dismissed immediately. How can you think this way about someone so important and busy, and yet bending so low to kiss the grass?

Then she hears from below her.

"The show is about to end. Tell me when you are ready, but take your time. He is waiting."

Angel finds herself in a state of animation and expectation, and not in the mood to watch the screen any longer.

"I can go now. Is it far? I may not be able to take the long walk."

"I shall continue to carry you."

"No. You have carried me for too long. You need a rest. I shall walk myself."

"Do you know you are as light as a feather?"

I am light as a feather? Angel shakes her head in disbelief. I am light only because you are supporting my every move. She takes a look downwards for the last time. There lies Grandma Pig, gaunt as ever, breathing gently. Then there is a noticeable air outflow, like a skier pushing strongly on ice for the last time, before relaxing all control to the gentle down slope until she can be brought to a complete stop.

With full contentment, Angel looks all the way up, and joyfully shouts, as if at the beginning of an exciting trip: Let us go.

CHAPTER 9 PARADISE

It is an undulating trip. Up and down, down and up, in a backdrop of snowy mountains above a tropical paradise, even better than what she saw in Vancouver long ago. She feels so close to earth that she can feel the grass waves. It is like on a magnetic levitation train, kissing the ground without touching it. Wind whistles from all directions. Whistling from Master, whistling from the family kids who have yet to learn whistling, and Angel's own whistling which comes not out of her mouth. She can also hear from weeping guitars, from violins on an open field, and from harmonicas in school concerts. The sound blows softly into her ear. It is so soothing and so comforting that she closes her eyes slowly. Not a single thought is on her mind. It is a trip that should last for ever.

In front of the mirror door, she can see Grandma Pig, just like what she has left her. The knitted brow formerly on Grandma Pig is now as smooth as ever. Hers is a lean and fit figure, confident and assured, like a marathon runner on the starting line looking at fellow runners and at the distance.

"Come closer, my child."

"Am I in heaven?"

"Yes you are. God is my name."

"Am I still Angel?"

"What a good name! I would hate to change that."

"Why am I here?"

"You deserve to be here, more than most people. You would not remember it, but I sent you down. I cannot wait for you to be back. How have you been treated?"

"They are so cr...difficult."

It is with much difficulty that Angel swallows the cruel word just in time. She feels a swelling up her eyes. Then she contradicts herself.

"I mean, they are so nice, and so good to me. I am forever indebted to the family. They have given me the best life, better than what I would ever have asked for as a pet. Most of them are nice, but some are like cruel tyrant when they treat us animals and their own women. They get nothing out of this cruelty. It does not make sense"

"I know."

"I have always been difficult to get along with. I am stubborn—what they call pig-headed. I ask too many questions. I am ungrateful when I am not satisfied."

"Pig-headed means differently here. You have a good head on your shoulder. Listen to me carefully, my child. Don't ever blame yourself for what you are. You should be proud of yourself. I am proud of you. If only there are more like you."

"I am not complaining, Sir, but they have invented crazy reasons to make us suffer so much."

"That is why I send you down."

"Their law is unfair to us, but I can understand that."

"We do not have such law here."

"Is it God's law?"

"It used to be called that. Now it is called heaven's law. Sounds better, eh? I am not the only one around here. I do not dictate everything, as some of them may believe."

"I do not know one bit about your, I mean, heaven's law. They say it is perfect."

"It is. If it is not, we change it to make it perfect. The law is there to make everybody happy, that is all."

"Sir, may I ask just one question? Can heaven's law apply on earth?"

"I have entrusted them with their free will; I have promised them my patience. They should know where the path will lead to. It is up to them to build the path and make their own law. I am not a micro-manager."

"Yet they have done such a terrible job."

"I know. It is much worse than I have expected."

"They say you are infallible."

"It may be a flattery, but it is true. I have my regrets. I wish things would have turned out better and faster."

If you regret, does it not mean that you have made a mistake? You regret the disappointing development, not the final outcome. Given the opportunity, you would still make the same decision. Hence it is not a mistake.

"Have you stopped their flattery?"

"Let me give you an example of harmful flattery. They claim to be my servants, and they blame me for the terrible things they have done, on me as their Lord. I must admit that I hate to be addressed as Lord, because this would reduce them as my serfs. I would appreciate you not calling me Master too. You are not my pet. I would rather not have flattery stronger than glorifying the word 'he' with a capital H, since it involves no more than a grammatical mistake. Name starts with a capital letter. God starts with a capital G. Canada starts with a capital C. Why does heaven not start with a capital H? I guess they must have some mix-up with flattery, which induces vanity and can be very dangerous. Their original sin arises from vanity."

God is apparently turning sombre. This is not the right time to press on with human failure, but Angel cannot suppress the boggling question on her mind. God may have immense patience, but surely there must be a limit to toleration. I wonder when and if that patience would be stretched to the limit, to the extent that God may say at last: enough is enough. Some say promises are made to be kept, and some say made to be broken. Please, God. The answer is blowing in the wind.

"Have you tried to interfere when things have gone too wrong? I mean, have you tried giving them a helping hand?"

"Of course I have. That is why I sent you, and those before you. I can also assure that you will not be the last. Don't think I am just sitting on my hands! It makes me sick to the bone to see what they are doing to themselves and to others."

Angel thinks of the professor. She looks up to God who is staring at her softly. There is a strong similarity in both, but yet there is a distinct difference. Both are important, and helpful to the extent of being generous. Both will lend a helping hand before you ask. What distinguishes God from the professor is compassion, which she cannot see in the professor. Compassion is so infused in God that he would not be God without it.

"Take your time. There is no hurry. Ask me any question, Child. Do not be afraid or shy."

"Have you regretted sending me? I may have done no harm, but at the same time I have not done anything at all."

"You have done more than I can expect, much more. I can tell you right now that you have accomplished your mission beyond my expectation. Let me tell you a little secret. Your story would be told. A movement will follow, possibly even under your name. Some yet to be born would wish they have met you."

I have achieved something? I don't think I have changed the world one bit. Is he doing harmless flattery on me? I must remind myself never to let vanity take over. I must always remain humble.

"Let me tell you another secret about a mission I regret. The remorse is still with me, and probably will never go away, even though it happened thousands of years ago. It is the first mission. I sent a young man."

"Do you mean that the first mission is not successful?"

"It is successful, but at what price? I know he would suffer terribly. It was unfair to him, and he would be hesitant to meet his fate, but his suffering is necessary to lead them back. I have never expected his suffering would be repeated so many times by those after him. I know beforehand what was going to happen to him. I know the destination of the path that he has started, but I do not expect building that path can involve so much torture and injustice. It is almost too much to make the mission worthwhile."

Angle can clearly find contortion in God's face. He is trying hard to hold back glistening tears crawling out of the corner of his eyes. How can he be as weak as a lamb? Yet the strength in that weakness can be so persuasive and commanding.

She feels a strong urge to hold him in her lap. What can she say?

"Do not cry."

"It is all right. Cry out all you can, if it can make you feel better."

"It is not your fault. You have done all you can."

Angel finds God staring into infinity at the same time as he speaks softly.

"They are learning, and they will continue to learn. Look on the bright side. I am almost sure they will not burn witches alive anymore in my name, not in that massive scale anyway."

God's face is lightening up, like some silver lining rimming a dark cloud.

"I must admit sending the first mission hesitantly. They call it the first coming, and they have been expecting the second coming ever since. They may not know it, but the second means all those after the first. There are many second comings. Yours is just one of them. Ever heard of DaVinci, farm girl Jeanne d'Arc, and the Chinese guy who claimed to be my second son?"

Angel has never heard of this Chinese guy.

"Is he really your second son?"

"There is no point to establish a numerical order after the first. You are my sons and daughters. All of you are. Human and animal, you are my children."

"What did he do?"

"He led a peasant revolt to establish the Pacific Celestial Kingdom, in an attempt to bring in my kingdom on Earth. The kingdom brought in good ideas of gender equality, unbound feet for woman, and so on, but it was brutally crushed by the corrupt imperial government, supported by the invading imperialist interest of Great Britain and France. Woman's bound feet would remain for nearly one hundred years more."

"They keep asking about these second comings, but I shall be prudent enough not to let them know when, before, or after. I have learnt my lesson. Causing seismic shock may not be suitable, since it will bring abrupt changes and excessive overreaction."

"Let me ask you a question. Answer if you like. Of all others available, why would you have chosen me, an uneducated pig? Surely there must be a better choice."

"The young man before you is no more educated. It is not my practice to send the strong and forceful. I shall never send a king or a professor."

"How can they be saved by someone weak and ignorant?"

"It is up to them to save themselves. The innocent among them will show the way. I shall only save their destiny collectively, though I do care for them individually. I have given them free will. They should not lie idly by, extending a hand for me to pull them up from sinking. They have the power to float, and they must exert their own effort."

"We are your people. Are you not our shepherd?"

"Yes. Put it this way. A pig is an animal, but human is animal too. I am a shepherd to all animals. All animals are equal, though not equally powerful. It is never my intention to have the strong overpowering the weak. In this respect, the strong has more responsibility than the weak to exercise caution and compassion."

God told her that she is the first non-human animal ever sent as a second coming. "When will the next second coming be?"

"I am open to suggestion. Around here we do discuss and debate before making decision. We are all equal here."

God is now apparently in a jovial mood.

"Look up behind you. All the way up. Do you see that? It says: The buck stops here. I pinch that from a decent American president."

"Then there is this Frenchman talking about power corruption and absolute power corruption. It is a benchmark of their progress."

"The revolution that followed had terror spilled all over. They say a revolution eats its own children."

"I am neutral on revolutions. I prefer gradual progress. Some revolutions are necessary, but cruelty can never be justified."

"There is also this Frenchman, or Frenchwoman, who said: I may not agree with you, but I shall defend your freedom of expression with my life. Truly remarkable, don't you think? I cannot say it better."

"I am constantly prayed to, and I am there to share their suffering. But I do not micro-manage and answer prayer every time. To do so would amount to no less than interference and intervention. I hope they can understand that their own effort and good fortune matter more than prayers, unless in exceptional cases."

"People have prayed to me to pass examination, in gambling, and in fighting. I hope they do not waste their time on these cheap and disrespectful prayers. I do not entertain request for a free lunch. There is no need to thank me if they are lucky."

"Prayer is often no more than asking for favour. It would be more meaningful for me listening to their feeling and desire. In most cases, they can discover how to find the proper way out by themselves, and this would indeed be my advice."

"They have also tried to bribe me with contribution and promised contribution to my church or to charity. Then they thank me or blame me, depending on their luck. Such calculating moves to induce fulfilment are demeaning both to me and to themselves. They should know better than to ask me for a good return on investment of this nature. I am not like those gods as believed in some mythology. "

"People on both sides of a war pray to win against each other. Families pray to bring their soldiers home. They thank me for their prayer being fulfilled, but they should help and share grief with fallen families instead. They should remember other people's sons and daughters, husbands and wives, and fathers and mothers, who are equally worthy but have fallen."

"Sometimes I do answer prayers. How and when they would not understand, nor arrived at by their own reasoning."

God would have continued on his monologue forever, but for a signal to leave the room. When he returns, a broad smile is in his face.

"The crowd waiting for you is getting unruly. I am afraid there will be a riot if you don't leave right now. Among them are two little guys."

My Little Runaways! Angel cannot control herself from shouting out loud. There is not one day when I do not think of them. She shoots out a volley of questions, and she wants to be hit back by no less, right at her heart, but she knows she cannot wait, not even for a minute.

"They are here? How are they? Have they grown up? Would they recognise me? Who has been taking care of them?

God answers deliberately, and the answer is crisp.

"Young and cute as ever!"

It is not clear whether Angel has heard the answer, rushing as she is out of the room without saying goodbye. With her heart pounding in overdrive, her pace is immediately quickened to a sprint. Not a second to lose. She is slowed down for a moment from a voice behind her.

"Don't think I am finished with you yet. All those animals! You will be busy soon."

She does not seem to notice the remark at all. Hers is a one-track mind, when the single most important issue will overwhelm everything else. It is getting late. Dusk in the sky has never been so beautiful. Firework can be seen and heard in the distance. It must be Guy Fawkes Day. That is the day when Big Sister would be dressed up as a cute little angel with wings, and Little Brother would be in period wear with the name of Guy on his back. Children in small groups would go door to door, shouting 'trick or treat' to the frightened adults who would readily yield goodies of candy or chocolate. It is a day of avenge, when children will be on top. Guy Fawkes has shown them a good example, or rather, a bad example. Many children would prefer this day to Christmas when they better be good because Santa is coming to town. Angel's babies never had the chance to play 'trick or treat'. They were gone too soon.

Is Guy Fawkes out to avenge their refusal to carry out policies he considered essential, or is this intended as a very serious warning? Nobody knows, but he should have known well in advance that he would not be spared for such a heinous crime, whether successful or not.

What can he expect to gain from blowing up such a beautiful landmark on the Thames, and giving up his own life in the process? One theory is that this is no more than 'trick or treat' in a grand scale. He is after the treat, but the trick had to be made believable. He would not be as lucky as the kids who would invariably get the treat, even if they are impatient enough to play the trick. This he should be well aware of.

In present-day term, he would be labelled a terrorist, or at best a martyr. Yet they remember him fondly, even to the extent of having a day named after him. Kids would be encouraged to follow his bad example, and adults would celebrate his deed in parties and bars. It speaks volumes of where that noble country would place its value, not on what he is prepared to die for, but on how he is prepared to sacrifice himself. Indeed, very few now even want to know or care about his cause.

Guy Fawkes would expect himself to be caught, and be on trial for high treason. It can be that blowing up Parliament is a mean to an end. His focus may all along be the trial, in which the pubic and those in power would have to listen, whether they like it or not. He would be given the opportunity to wake them up, and he is ready to pay the price.

Angel imagines Guy Fawkes more sad than angry at the trial. Perhaps he would even be glad that Parliament has not been blown up after all. It is supposed to happen at night when no one would be killed, hopefully. After execution, his spirit may hover down from Tower Bridge, to see better days ahead because of him.

If his spirit is still around, he would have spotted the Thames River crossing closest to Parliament. Waterloo Bridge has a movie with the same name, which in Chinese is translated as Soul Broken at Blue Bridge. Blue Bridge? The movie is about a girl, played by Vivien Leigh, jumping down to die in the ever-flowing river at the end of the Second World War. The cruelty of lovers separating is replaced by the cruelty of social pressure. She does not want to disgrace her upper class veteran boyfriend. In her loneliness, someone should have persuaded her that she has not done anything degrading worse than a pig, or worse than any of those pretending to be on moral high ground. It is about social justice against prosecution, worth to die fighting for, but is it worth killing herself? I would say: No. Please don't.

Let me tell you: This is worse than gruesome murder.

I would like to see Guy Fawkes hovering around in her last moment. You will not die in vain. Your death will leave a footprint to the progress of human civilization, to a more tolerant world.

Why should she feel ashamed? Why does she not wait until after the last meeting with her lover? Why does he stand on the bridge all alone, years later, looking for her face in the wrinkled water? The social pressure is too much. Waiting can only makes things worse.

Fast forward that Vivien girl or her spirit. Let her be an audience rather than an actress in a movie-house. Invite her to see Jamie Lee Curtis in Trading Places in 1983, Julia Roberts in Pretty Woman in 1990, and Kim Basinger in L.A. Confidential in 1997. Perhaps she would not have jumped, and we audience can come home sweet with a happy ending. Really? It is all a matter of timing? We should believe it.

We may be tempted to criticize past script writers and audience for their lack of empathy on hookers, particularly those shy ones like desperate Vivien, and we may blame the past failure to see them beyond the moralistic claptrap, but this is unfair. Let us leave ourselves alone to enjoy an old movie with new feelings of sorrow and sadness, and let us have our anger and frustration lingering on.

They would not listen. They did not know how. Perhaps they listen now.

Perhaps they never will.

In her radical youth, soon after the vision where she met her lifetime intellectual soul-mate, Angel has been busy all summer, mining inside the shed behind the fence. This shed has seen Master graduating from trial-and-error handyman to woodworker to clock repairer to apprentice sculptor. It has heard New Year resolutions, broken promises, and long-forgotten commitments. There were even hugs and kisses, endearment, and quarrels. Lying on the corner of the worktable is a half-empty ashtray with a dead fly close by. Hanging on and above the tabletop are scattered tools and a metal leg. Fine machine parts are scattered on the rest of the table. If the shed can talk and you will listen, it can tell you many stories of sweet dream and disappointment, failure and success, altered plans, and even achievement. But Angel is too busy to afford the time. She is digging. She has been digging all summer, and with autumn approaching the work is almost done. It is hard work, though, and very dangerous too. A coalminer of yesteryears would certainly reject such a job offer. It is hard enough crawling in through the mountain of cardboard boxes. Below a pinup unfinished Sudoku sheet, precariously-hung screw-drivers and hammers aim and scheme to drop any time with best effect. The working space is tight and suffocating. It is amazing how anyone can stay there for more than a few minutes, but Angel is on a self-appointed mission. She has assigned herself, and she is the only one to know. She is the world's loneliest terrorist, in the role of both giving and receiving instruction. She is dedicated and unstoppable.

I shall blow up the slaughter house. The idea is struck after a walk outside the slaughterhouse front yard, with doubled-over bottled gas tanks. If she can knock them down, the leaking gas will start an explosion, and the slaughterhouse will be blown to smithereens. She would sneak out in the dead of night, out of the house through that tunnel. She may even bring a live fuse along to make sure it happens. Then she has a better idea, an inspiration from the evening news. All she has to do to make her body the live fuse. It is that simple. Chew up the wires, and jump in between the two ends. In a minute, the slaughterhouse will be history. What happens to her she cares not.

But she does care, and that is the trouble. She cares not so much for herself as for others. She has not what it takes to be a terrorist. Her trouble can be summarized by one word: Compassion. It is what would do her in, like a stealthy worm creeping in ever so gently as to entirely escape notice. The worm then takes a steady hold, bite by bite. By the time you are aware, it is already too late. As gluey as sticky glue, once it is on you, it will be on you forever. You try to take it off? Forget it. It is a cancer, an enemy that survives and thrives on whatever it can feed on, an enemy that has turned itself to be a part of you, to the extent that you will not know who you are fighting against. It is the worst fight in the world. You are fighting against yourself.

The trouble starts innocently enough. Angel is aware right from the beginning that all inside the slaughterhouse will be a part of that glorious conflagration. No pain, no gain, as the professor has said. I shall end their misery. The pain they suffer will be instant, and much less than being slaughtered one by one. I am their saviour, though this is not my concern, and they will never know me. That is right. They will never know what has happened, and they will not know what is about to happen, for obvious reasons.

Angel compares herself with them. I have a comfortable life, and I shall live on for many years to come. They have only a few days more to live, or at most a week or so. Time is of the essence. What matters is that they will be slaughtered painfully, and there is not one single thing they can do to prevent it, except by my action. Angel can see herds after herds being driven into the slaughterhouse. Diverse herds, each varying in number from a few to tens. Individuals and families, they all know what is going to happen. Parents, with tears in their eyes, would comfort the kids. It is alright. We are going to a picnic. Mom would take care of everything. Be patient. It is fun ahead.

No more of this, once I get rid of the slaughterhouse for good, so Angel thinks. A few days more for them to live means nothing, especially when the time is spent in tormenting anticipation, except for the kids who can be persuaded by lies. Then one question creeps in. If a few days do not matter, will a few weeks matter, and will a few years matter? Hey, you must have a sense of proportion. What if it is indeed a few years? Would you like to prolong their suffering any longer? What is there in life if it is not worth living? Come on.

The temporary calm that comes with this thinking does not last. The hydra of compassion has many heads. Who are you to shorten their lives abruptly? Who do you think you are please? Sisters may want to say goodbye to brothers, and parents to their off-springs. They may have made plans for their last days, which may be the most meaningful, even if not the happiest. Even if you can notify every one of them, who are you to force your decision on them? The lives are theirs, not yours. Sure, you have a noble cause, but your cause is not necessarily their cause. You can sacrifice yourself for what you may want to believe in, as long as it does not affect me. If it does, can you please first ask me? I deserve your respect too.

The sticky glue has stuck. The more Angel tries to get rid of it, the stickier it becomes. She is hopelessly caught. Then Guy Fawkes Day comes, as a strong inducement for action regardless, at the same time as it worsens the debacle. Guy Fawkes was arrested. I wonder what happened to him and his family. If I have been arrested or found dead, I would have brought trouble to my human family too. I am sorry. You have been treating me so well, and all I can bring you is nothing but trouble.

The day ends with the family bringing in leftover memorabilia at the end of day, things that they will throw away as garbage soon. Angel is shocked to read what is written on the tattered posters. "Come back. All is forgiven." She instantly feels relief so complete as to collapse right away. So they have forgiven him, and he has forgiven them? Do they just let him go because there is no burning? Please do not let it end like that. Give him a trial. It is the least he deserves after all that. Do not let all his effort go in vain. Listen to him please.

What if they still find his talk rubbish? It is alright. The important thing is to listen and to consider. They can take their sweet time to work it out. Thinking it out is more than half way there. On the other hand, if they can influence him enough to change his mind, it is fine too. Guy is a noble soul. Execution or not, it matters little. If only I can be as brave as he is, and if the rest of us are, the world will be a better place.

That is one of those rare nights when Angel cannot be happier. The thought swirls round and round in circles. Her heart is so full that she has to press it with both her hands to keep it from bursting. In bed, she weeps so silently that not a sound can be heard. I am happy for you. I am happy for your humankind. I am happy for all the animals in the world.

She cannot remember when she falls asleep. It is a long night that seems to last forever. The next morning she finds her pillow soaking wet. Mistress is surprised by her swollen eyes but is no told why. She would keep that night a secret until her dying days.

That is about the end of her terrorist phase, but it is not a happy ending. The slaughterhouse continues to receive its fill, as she continues to have her fill of sorrow and remorse. Why did I not do what I could have done? Is it too late to start anew? Should I join them at the slaughterhouse? But her mind is soon swept away with pregnancy, which comes to have its mellowing effect. With the piglets' arrival, she no longer thinks of going to the slaughterhouse. Everything has to be delayed for the future. Those little rascals always try to run away. The louder you call, the faster they run away in the opposite direction. They are hopeless. It is not as if one rascal is trouble enough for me. There have to be two. I call them runaways. They are My Little Runaways.

Angel recovers from her thoughts to find herself going towards the firework. Could the firework be for me? Do not call it Angel Day, please. I have hardly done anything to deserve that. Let it remain as Guy Fawkes Day, or Martyr Day if you insist. To join the celebration would be good enough for me.

She closes her eyes, allowing her legs to carry the distance. When she reopens them, she can hardly see through the mist in front of her. The salty taste, from her sweat and tear, is so good that she would not swallow any drop before savouring. Suddenly she notices that she is no longer angry. How long since has it gone she does not know, but she is no longer angry at the slaughterhouse, at the two men in the blood red van, and even at impregnable and inscrutable human tyranny. It seems her anger has been melted away completely. Did God say that suffering has been banished? She will ask for a favour next time: Banish anger. Let there be no anger again, here, there, and anywhere.

She looks up. There is a banner across the gate in front. There is a big crowd beneath stretching some way back up the gentle slope. There are humans, animals, and even dogs, but most of all there are two little guys up front. There are so many of them, that most must be strangers. Have they all been standing there waiting for her, or are they waiting for someone else? She looks up, but with her misty eyes against the light, she cannot read it. Maybe the banner is not for her. Maybe the banner does no have her name on. Suddenly she has a wish. Banner, please do not say: Welcome Back, Angel. Please do not treat me as a heroine. I am welcoming you as much as you are welcoming me. Let me first of all welcome my Little Runaways. Let them run towards me. Let them run faster the louder I call. Don't ever run away from Mama again.

This must be Guy Fawkes Day. Now is their chance dressing up to play: Trick or Treat? I should have come earlier. There is no time. Firework has already started. I hope someone would have dressed them up for me. I cannot wait to see what they look like. Maybe they will shout at me: Trick or Treat, Mom? I would be so scared as to yield immediately. Then I would take both of them up, and I would hug them so tight that all air will be squeezed out, and nothing but sweet goodies will be left.

She wonders who else will be waiting. Would her human family members be around? Would she see Big Sister and Little Brother? Would she see companion Mistress and handyman Master? Then she thinks of others. Would she see Anne Boleyn, Madame Rolland, Jeanne, William Wallace, young Lenin's elder brother, Guy Fawkes, the Dalai Lama, and the Political Bureau? What would she say to them? Should it be: let us listen to one another, let there be peace, and let us follow

God's example of immense patience, tolerance, and most important of all, compassion.

She looks up for the last time. The words in the banner are now discernable. Slowly she mumbles out the words one by one, as if unwilling to let each word slip away. Yes, this is exactly what I want, everywhere, on Earth and in heaven.

The words in the banner reads: 'Come Back. All Is Forgiven.'

CPSIA information can be obtained at www.ICGtesting.com
Printed in the USA
BVOW05s1113180914

367402BV00001B/81/P

9 781451 279672